To Judy

OF DICE AND MEN

A BRACKENBOOKS PUBLICATION
TORONTO

This is a work of fiction. All the characters, organizations, and events portrayed in this novel are either products of the author's imagination or are used fictitiously.

OF DICE AND MEN

Top Cover Photograph is a cropped version of "IMG_9147" by Jo Amelia Finlay Bever, used under the CC BY 2.0 license
Bottom Cover Photograph by Brackenbooks
Cover Design by Brackenbooks

Edited by Brackenbooks

Published by Brackenbooks.
Toronto, Ontario

www.oliverbrackenbury.com

ISBN: 978-1-73141-150-1 (Paperback)

First Edition: November 2018

Special Thanks to

CHILDHOOD PETS

They're pretty great, except when they aren't.

(Luckily, mine was!)

Of Dice and Men

PART ONE

"So, is she hot?"

"Greg's sister? Eh..."

Kendra hid in the upstairs bathroom's door frame, listening to her brother's friend's talking in the living room. She hadn't put up too much of a fight when Greg, taking advantage of their parents being out, insisted Kendra's bedtime was nine o'clock. She knew he wanted to feel free to discuss girls and sex and things with his guy pals; a prime opportunity for her to learn salacious gossip and other valuable information. She certainly hadn't expected the conversation to turn to her, but when her brother had to go retrieve the family canine, Salvador Doggy, who'd once again escaped the backyard to go adventuring, her brother's friends seized the opportunity to discuss his sister.

It would have been bad enough if the tall one, Steve, had stopped with "Eh...", but he didn't. "Spaghetti legs, spaghetti arms, not much ass, not much tits - perky though, like they're happy to see you."

Equal parts grossed out and fascinated, she held tightly in place, mindful of her size elevens stretching into the hallway. Kendra doubted her breasts would ever be happy to see Steve. Despite herself, she glanced down to assess their status. It would have been easier to dismiss his words if he was ugly, but he wasn't. More than once Kendra had wanted to tuck in the tag of his shirt, if only for an excuse to feel his neck.

Steve continued: "Hair like a librarian, which makes her look nerdier, and an okay face if you're not bothered by big glasses and a permanent retainer. Kind of a medium face."

"Dude," she heard Eric reply, probably gesticulating wildly with his large hands the way she'd seen him do so often, "Why are you being so wordy?"

Yeah, jerk. Kendra thought.

"Don't you have a picture from when you all went to the beach?" the third one, Phil, asked, his voice cracking on 'trip'. She convinced herself their guffaws were at the absurdity of his giving a long description when he could have just shown the picture, despite what the quiet between Phil's question and the peals of laughter suggested.

"So," Steve again, "would you fuck her?"

Kendra darted across the hall into her bedroom, failed to shut the door quietly and tossed herself at the bed so hard it was if she was trying to break through to another world, a dimension where she'd never have to hear the answer. Wrapping a pillow around her ears, she just managed to block out the replies to Steve's question. She tried to think of something less stressful, of the film she'd watched with her mother the night before: Annie Hall.

The scene her mind went back to was when six-year-old Alvy was chastised for kissing a girl in his class, and for having an interest in kissing at such a young age. Kendra understood where

Alvy was coming from, but was careful never to mention this to anyone other than her closest friend, Val, since this upset most adults even more when coming from a girl. Her favorite parts of the film came after that scene. Diane Keaton's iconic men's shirt, vest, tie, and hat. Everyone, who was supposed to be respected, reading books. No man-children or princesses, even among the dummies who were there to be laughed at. These were sophisticated city dwellers for whom sex was important, but no big deal.

Casual. Casual sex. The casual having and discussing of sex. Yup, no big deal, not for someone cultured and full of witty & profound things to say. What came first, the sex or the class with which they had it? Whatever it was, while sex might not solve all their problems, Kendra always imagined these 1970's, trendy, clever New Yorkers as being empowered and enriched by their bedroom experiences. Sex didn't make anybody lose anything or leave the women used, broken, dirty and so on, like it did in any number of cruel, moralizing tales. It was food for thought, gave the sparkle to their auras of worldliness, and unlocked the door to a life Kendra wanted so badly it often overwhelmed her. She assumed there was a time where she hadn't thought about sex. The closest she could remember, though, was before she understood what sex actually entailed; when she'd thought it was somewhere between hugging and sumo wrestling. A visiting aunt must have sensed something or else why, years ago, did she give Kendra a box of old paperbacks that looked innocent enough but all had pages dog-eared at some really steamy parts?

Looking over at a stack of those very paperbacks on her

bedside table, Kendra vowed she would lose her virginity before turning sixteen. To touch and be touched was so important to her, she couldn't bear the thought of forever failing to connect with someone on that level. There'd been some very chaste middle-school moments, and a mishap in grade one that made a former friend's parent banish her from ever visiting again, but none of that counted. She knew if she didn't make her goal, it would mean she was forever inferior to those who had. She certainly knew she needed to have sex before high school was over, or be doomed to a lifetime membership in an inescapable underclass of People Who Lost It Too Late Or Maybe Never. Kendra decided if by then she was still a virgin it wouldn't matter if she became bright, witty, and stylish in a way that was entirely her own, she'd still be a hollow version of who she wanted to be, living on the fringes of who shw wanted to be accepted by. If that happened…Kendra didn't know what she'd do.

When the muffled trumpet noises of boy-chatter died down enough to make her feel safe, she let the pillow's two ends flap down from her head like Salvador Doggy's ears when he'd throw himself on his back to solicit a tummy rub. She knew it was wrong for them to talk about her, about anybody, like they had. Kendra wanted to go out and tell them off, but what if that just fed into the perception of her as an ugly, humorless "librarian"? How much harder would it be to hear those horrible things said to her face?

Glancing at her phone's slender white form for just long enough, she thumbed her way to one of the first albums she hadn't discovered in her parent's vinyl collection. Kendra slid a large pair of headphones on in the pillow's place, their padded sides even softer and, focusing on the music, closed her eyes.

Once she was sure her pupils had adjusted, she opened her eyes wide and enjoyed how much darker her room seemed. When she was very little she'd sworn this trick allowed her to see fuzzy, indistinct creatures calmly plodding across her bedroom floor. These semi-transparent, flickering fellows meant well, she was sure. Any dangerous monsters lived in the basement, naturally, and could be briefly held at bay by a pair of extended middle fingers.

There weren't any creatures under her desk by the window looking out over their front lawn, none around the beanbag chair nestled in the corner with her bookshelves, and the only creatures on the shelves were little plastic ones she'd collected for as long as she could remember. Oh well.

What if Steve was as nice as he was good-looking?

Kendra turned her eyes to the ceiling, her dilated pupils seeing a richer, creamier darkness. Reaching downward, she painted images across this black canvass, of being alone with Steve on a desert island; pressing her other pillow between her legs, hoping what was supposed to happen finally would; careful not to tongue the cross-wire of her permanent retainer, lest it cut through the fantasy.

Between Thumb and Index Finger

Thin rubber soles flapped loudly on the oval track, sometimes slapping down an errant tuft of grass pushing up between reddish-brown gravel. Shafts of light cut across the field, inching further and further from between nearby trees. Their spacing was almost even, making Kendra smile as she felt the sun's warmth pass over her in regular intervals.

Greg never did find Salvador Doggy. Breakfast had an air of tension left over from when their parents had put him on blast the night before. They'd told him he wasn't allowed to have friends visit until the dog was found, and he was still sour about it in the morning. Kendra wasn't too pleased with him either. Even though they were in a safe neighborhood and Salvador had taken short trips like this before, she found herself running her finger up and down the spine of an Alice Munro novel; regretting every occasion she'd chosen to do something other than take him for a walk; wishing she'd ignored Greg's nonsense bedtime to help look for Salvador; wondering if the last time she'd seen him had been The Last Time. It was so difficult to imagine life without this little companion who'd joined the family before her second birthday. She knew she could find him, could solve this, if she had even one decent clue to start with. It was maddening to be so full of energy and not know where to put it.

Kendra willed her finger to stop fraying the book's spine, knowing her stress would infect her mom if it wasn't hidden better. Soon her Dad would, on his way to a shift at the moving company, give her a ride to school. Her mother teased her for not 'being a real teenager' because of her waking up early, so she could run before classes started. Kendra began to answer, but was distracted by the sound of her brother coming downstairs. He slouched through the kitchen, reached into the middle of the table and took the last slice of toast just before Kendra's fingers made contact.

"Greg, you suck!" Kendra shouted to the sky.

"Uh, hey." Kevin replied.

"Ohyeah,heyGreg'smyBROTHERandhesucks." Speaking quickly never did seem to head off embarrassment at the pass. Kendra's early morning goosebumps got goosebumps, Kevin had run up alongside her so quietly. Red shorts with white piping. Black undershirt showing off tanned arms with soft blond hairs running back from strong wrists. Sharp, blue eyes. Highly acceptable.

Kendra had often admired his body; the person piloting it was mostly a mystery. Though they'd gone to the same middle school, he'd only been another blob in the mass of boys who she had nothing in common with and no desire to get to know. That changed at the start of this, their first year of high school, when she'd noticed how much his skin had absorbed the summer sun. A Basic Boy with a shine of burgeoning manliness was just what Kendra fancied, a good starter model, a Practice Boy for her to get a feel for new feelings, the act of feeling, and being felt up. After an amicable split, she'd be able to move on to her first big love without feeling completely clueless. Kevin had never dated anybody either, as far as she knew, so they'd both be doing each other a favor.

First he had to take a liking to her. Kendra figured she just had to get him thinking about the sexy side of life while in her company and biology would take care of the rest. Remembering a little of his interests, overheard while eavesdropping in the halls, she cobbled together a plan and put it into motion.

"I didn't expect to see you here this morning," she lied.

"What? I always run before school starts."

"Oh, ha, yeah." She laughed in a way she hoped was appealing.

Not sure how to read his reaction, Kendra wondered if she should think more about how she laughed. Plus, oh hey, they were still running beside each other? Did she drop back a bit? Pull ahead? If she stayed in position she'd have to say something and, here in the moment, her plan didn't feel as perfect as it had before. He was looking at her. Shit.

"So, uh."

"Hey, you wanna hear something crazy?" She said. He shrugged, rolling those shoulders of his as if to say he could go either way. Kendra began breathing a little heavier.

"You know how your favorite movie is The Godfather?"

He gave one clear, affirmative nod.

"Well okay, so have you read the book?" One firm, declarative head shake.

"Oh man, you should. There's all kinds of stuff which didn't make it into the movie. Like, uh..."

Kendra glanced around to see if anybody else was going to pop up beside them. In the distance people were starting to cluster around the school entrances, a few of her gaming pals were sitting in a circle on wet grass far from everyone else, and the familiar silhouette of her best friend, Valory, could be seen approaching. She wondered if Val would get to see Kevin ask her our or pat her on the butt or *something*.

"You remember the big wedding at the start, right?" She continued, "Well there's this one scene in the kitchen of the Godfather's big ol' mansion where a bunch of the wives are talking. They're gossiping, of course, and eventually the wife of Sonny Corleone – you know, the really angry son who gets shot to death at the toll booth?"

"Hey, spoilers!" Kevin grinned.

"You said it's your favorite! Besides, you can't say 'spoiler' about anything more than ten years old, that's the rule." This felt good, she'd rarely seen Kevin smile before, "So yeah, Sonny Corleone's wife starts talking and it's all about how Sonny has just a total horse dick."

A little embarrassed, Kendra stared ahead while telling Kevin about this and more; spitting it out as fast as she could, now she was committed. Describing the bridesmaid, who was "uh, a little big down there", pursuing Michael Corleone in the wedding scene, she had more and more trouble seeing how sharing this tale of a "perfect fit" might lead to something warm and pleasant happening between her and Kevin. Soon she wished she didn't feel compelled to provide every single detail. Confidence in her gambit began to fall away like bolts and bits from a ramshackle go-cart, its driver keeping the accelerator pressed down, trying to outrun their own ruin.

This was followed by a pause at least as long as Michael Corleone's member.

"Did you memorize that?" Kevin said. Back at Kendra's house a well-thumbed copy of The Godfather, the spine cracked in line with a particular place in its narrative, sat on her bedroom floor between two tall stacks of Teen Titans Go! comic books her dad had given her from his collection. On the schoolyard, Val reached the edge of the track.

"See you later!" Kendra called to Kevin, running straight to her friend.

After a quick exchange of pleasantries while walking back towards the school building, Kendra decided to share what just happened with her friend, only to be interrupted when Valory gestured back to the track and said, "Look, that nutjob Mary is trying to talk to Kevin."

Neither of them really knew much about Mary other than she was tall, came from a poor family, and there were rumors of her acting weird sometimes; like how she actually cried when a field of sunflowers was paved over for a parking lot and still got upset if someone reminded her. The girls knew it wasn't right to look down on or make fun of Mary, but their guilt from doing so couldn't compete with the relief of being able to channel the river of schoolyard snark downward, through themselves, instead of being drowned by it. For Kendra, it didn't hurt that Mary was running alongside Kevin in her track clothes from Goodwill and did, in fact, seem to be deploying her go-to move - staring like a total goon at the object of her affection.

Kendra, about to slather on some snark, caught herself and sighed.

"Whatever, she can take a shot. It's not like I didn't totally screw up with him just now." Kendra told the tale of two minutes ago. Valory laughed. Kendra wrapped up by saying "I guess my quest for two butts has reached its conclusion. Which is a shame because, like, 'Kevin and Kendra', right?"

"Two butts?"

"I wasn't just running to chase some stupid boy." Kendra clapped one hand on her behind, "This isn't gonna grow itself, so I figured if I took up running..."

"God, you want curves so bad? I'll lend you some of mine." Valory offered, pinching at an offending cheek with one hand while unceremoniously squeezing a plump breast with the other, "You know my mom will only buy me, like, two bras because she says they cost so much? Black and nude, that's all I got."

"Only two bras, but how many boys look at you?"

Valory opened her mouth to reply, swiftly switching to a sneer. Following her friend's eye-line, Kendra noticed Paul had walked over from the circle of her gaming pals. Some part of his inner programming had told him just standing behind her and waiting until she turned around had been the way to join the conversation. Even though Valory had been touching herself with all the sensuality of shoving an irritating pet off the couch, Paul was staring. Kendra decided to save him from himself.

"Hey Paul!" she said, moving to block his view. She still needed to tug on one of his many buckles. Paul had recently switched from hand me downs to a collection of black jeans, t-shirts, and socks which were topped off with a floor length coat carrying an over-abundance of said buckles. Kendra had yet to make her own upgrade, still not knowing what she wanted to look like when she burst out of her grade school fashion cocoon.

"Ah. Hello Kendra. Sorry, I didn't want to interrupt. Are you still coming out tonight?"

"For sure! Your place at seven, right?"

"Yes. Don't forget your character. I could print another copy, I suppose, however it wouldn't have any of your notes on it."

"I'll bring some Pepsi, too. Can all the other guys make it?"

"Well," Paul sniffed, "Richard's going to be late, because Richard, and Tim might not make it until eight-thirty, depending on if his family has dinner at an appropriate time."

"Ugh, God, I know right?" Kendra agreed, "Six o'clock is dinnertime, not seven." Feeling Valory tugging on her elbow, she wrapped things up and the two girls headed indoors. As they passed through, the ambient conversations of almost a thousand students flowed around them, escaping across the wet grass of the field.

Standing by the entrance to the gymnasium, Kendra decided to try barking up the wrong tree for the tenth time or so. "You know Val, you really should-"

"I'm not into role-playing games, no way, no how." Val raised her open hands high, "Why are you always trying to get me into that stuff?"

"It's fun!" Riffing off her friend, Kendra threw her hands up in the air like a theme park mascot trying to work a crowd, "And because it'd be cool," her hands flopped down to her sides, "to not be the only girl."

Being late felt like losing a game of musical chairs where the penalty was getting grief from the teacher. Noticing some kids were starting to head for their homerooms, they put the conversation on hold, Valory heading off to her classroom while Kendra ducked in to use the girls' changing room.

Stepping up to the locker she'd claimed earlier, Kendra was glad the early morning air had been cool enough to keep her from sweating. Not having to shower didn't just save time, it helped minimize the chance of being teased for her unruly pubes. She was both grossed out and envious so many girls in her year were already trimming down there, creating a landscape that wouldn't poke out from the narrow crotches of underwear which was always, always designed with an assumption of diligent gardening. After one changing room encounter, Kendra had to have her mother explain how the other girls hadn't been born that way and Kendra didn't have a "Chew-crack-a", as one girl referred to it. She wondered if her mother regretted clearing this up when, maybe an hour later, she'd found her daughter in the bathroom using a pair of scissors with all the finesse of a jungle explorer clearing a path.

In the present, Kendra arranged her pair of hand me down boy's jeans so she could hop into them, after sliding off her running shorts, as quick as possible. Satisfied nobody else was around, she executed her well-practiced maneuver.

"Hey Kendra."

It was her other girlfriend, Gwen Senger. Kendra was distracted from concern about what Gwen might have seen by the thought that if she could just be really nice to a bunch of people then maybe the universe would reward her with getting to touch Kevin's butt. That's how karma works, right? Probably. That's probably how it works.

"Oh, hey Gwen!" Kendra knew why her friend was in the changing room. Gwen's mom kept a strict, conservative dress code for her daughter. This lead to the junior Senger building an entire secret wardrobe, paid for with her summer job as a camp counselor, which she changed into each morning at school.

"Did you see Kevin when you ran this morning?"

"Yeah. I kind of messed up I think, which is a shame because man...I mean, you know, dude has size fourteen shoes."

Gwen, switching a shapeless sweater for a cherry red halter top, performed an exasperated sigh at Kendra's lack of worldly knowledge.

"Kendra, that whole shoe size to penis size ratio thing doesn't work." she said, beginning to demonstrate the correct method, "You gotta get the guy to stick his thumb out sideways and then look at the distance from where it meets his palm to the tip of his index finger."

"Ohhhh." Kendra finished tightening her belt to the hole her mom had had to punch just before the first one. Gwen may have started to get a little full of herself since losing her virginity the previous summer, but she was a prime source of information Kendra would never skim from listening in on her older brother and his pals. She still couldn't believe Gwen had had sex at age thirteen. Even knowing this was unusual, it still increased the pressure she'd recently found herself feeling, like suddenly being deep beneath the sea.

Everyone around her, and most of what she absorbed from fiction and media, told Kendra it was easy for any woman to lose her virginity. She wasn't so sure. A question for Gwen started to form and then the homeroom bell rang, chasing the thought from her head and the two girls out of the changing room.

Role-Playing Games

Kendra came down the basement stairs of Paul's house to see the three boys around a folding card table whose green felt had been peeled back in places by idle fingernails. Yellows, oranges, and reds of pulverized snack food were ground into the edges still glued on, creating a fiery patina of chemical flavoring. Pop cans, full and empty, were clustered in front of each player, haphazardly arranged around precious pieces of eraser-smudged paper like so many aluminum bodyguards. A three-paneled piece of cardboard stood in front of Paul and his notes, screening them from everyone else, with tables of rules on the back and wild illustrations of Teutonic titans tearing through a mosaic of maniacal monsters on the front. They'd only started playing the previous summer, yet entire civilizations had been built, saved, and destroyed on this crucible of conflict, this table.

"Dude, shift over." Paul said to Richard.

"No way, I was the first one here, so I get the best seat." Richard replied, "I'm never the first one here."

"Sure, I guess we don't have to play today." Paul said under his breath, taking a slug of Pepsi for punctuation.

Kendra, crossing cold grey carpet while admiring a column of National Geographic magazines stacked from floor to slightly sunken ceiling, heard their exchange and didn't pay much attention. It was a familiar script. One of these days she was going to set Paul straight over his insistence on her getting special treatment when they all hung out. Right now, Kendra didn't want to taint the mood any more than Paul already had, so she tried to think about other things than Richard grimacing as he sat down upon a hard wooden stool with no back support for his gangly frame. Kendra also tried not to enjoy settling her bony butt into the plush red cushion of a high backed dining room chair Paul's father had picked up at a garage sale two weeks ago.

Her fingers flew as she set to filling the space made for her on the table with a slim white folder, a plastic cube filled with thirty-six green dice, two mechanical pencils, and an eraser with the logo of her father's work on it; a pale blue ink outline of a moving van above BRANSTON, the boss' last name. Kendra smiled. She'd been looking forward to this all week.

Her smile broke into a yawn.

"Tired much?" Richard asked, "You're always yawning."

"Kendra runs track every morning." Paul cut in, "Well, most mornings."

"Why would you do that?" Tim asked around the last chips from a bag of salt & vinegar.

"Because it's fun!" Kendra replied, "And, you know, exercise."

"Pfft, yeah, you're pretty fat there Kendra." Richard went for the other bag of chips.

"Haha, yeah well I cracked triple digits during the summer so I better watch myself." Kendra laughed, "I might even-"

"Uh, she's obviously not, Richard." Paul cut in again. Richard just stared at him. Tim looked off to the side, waiting for the conversation to move on.

"So yeah, okay, I didn't finish buying stuff from the merchant dude?" Kendra stated, opening the white folder to reveal a sheet with all the details for her character, Sing Sing; named so because she was playing a bard who was also such a good tracker nobody could ever escape her.

Well, Kendra thought it was cool.

Kendra also liked how her character's attributes, such as strength, intelligence and willpower, were measured in quantifiable number ranges. That being said, even though Kendra knew 'Body' in this game translated as how easily a character could shrug off damage, the remarks of her brother's friends left her feeling a little funny reading "Body: 4".

But whatever, there was plenty else on the page. Her character's excellent tracking skill both she and Kendra found any excuse to use, a beloved bejeweled dagger in her inventory, and several doodles in the margins. Kendra's favorite had come from when Richard, playing a wizard, had threatened to turn her legs into dicks if she didn't give him his share of gold from the hoard of a necromancer. Riffing on that, she'd doodled her character talking dirty to her dick-legs so they'd stay hard enough to walk on. Tim had then leaned over and created a second image in the sequence where Sing-Sing saw a naked old man, wandering in the street as they do, and become so grossed out her legs went flaccid - causing her to tumble down a flight of stairs she'd been climbing.

The game kicked off with Kendra buying some rations for the

journey ahead, and the mood shifted as Paul became lost in the improvisation of running the game. The next five hours flitted by as an abandoned dwarven mine was explored by Sing-Sing the bard, Grapenuts, Tim's orc barbarian, and Class War, Richard's elven sorcerer.

An hour later they all stared at Paul in rapt attention as he used his best dramatic narrator voice to relay the details of a rockslide triggered by the arrival of a gigantic magma worm. Riding atop the molten beast was Yidhra, an enemy they'd made in their first adventure. Back then she'd just been a meddling wife to the mayor of a town they were passing through. Now she was half-demon and hellbent for their blood, a terrible deal having been struck so she could have the power to take her revenge for the many times she'd been thwarted by the players. The battle gave their character's new scars, and the players themselves gained a story they'd all enjoy retelling to each other for years to come, as beloved as any inside joke or favorite scene from a film.

Wrapping up their exploration of the mines not a minute too soon, a firm period was placed at the evening's end by the loud thump of Paul's father giving three booming stomps on the floor above them; his signal he wanted the house cleared of noisy children.

"I heard you, father!" Paul shouted to the ceiling. Richard and Kendra gathered up their pencils and so on. Tim lingered.

"Paul, can we just handle my spending experience on some new skills?" he pleaded with Paul, "I think I have enough to go up a couple of points in Battle-Axe."

"I don't want to do that at the start of the next game, it slows everything down." Paul whispered, "Okay, we'll do it quickly and quietly."

Richard stifled his laughter and Kendra gave him a look to let him know she was on the same page. They took to the basement stairs, leaving Paul and Tim to do it quickly and quietly. Richard paused, letting Kendra go ahead, when Paul called to him in a stage whisper.

"Richard, it's late, are you going to walk Kendra home?"

"Well we live in the same direction." Richard replied, "I guess so."

"Excellent. You do as a gentleman should."

"Um, okay."

Satisfied, Paul looked down into a large rulebook. Upstairs, Kendra and Richard sought out their shoes from the swarm of sneakers by the door. Paul's mother watched, waiting to lock the door behind them. She didn't say anything the entire time, which totally wasn't weird at all.

Kendra felt her skin tighten in the cool Fall air. A total lack of cloud cover allowed some stars to peek through the light pollution as her and Richard turned left at the end of the driveway and started towards their respective homes. It took a few sighs, quiet looks into the distance, and small talk about school, but Richard found his way to bringing up the subject he wanted to discuss.

"Hey, uh, can I have the good seat next game? Like, if I get there before Tim, anyways?"

"Sure, and hey, you don't have to ask."

"Well yeah, but…"

"Yeah."

"My mom heard me bitching about it to Tim one time." Richard's shoulders tensed a little, "And she thinks Paul's intimidated by girls. But, I dunno."

Kendra leaned her head back, raising an eyebrow. "What? Girls aren't scary."

"To be fair, some of them are!"

"Like Stephanie? I'm not the same as her." Kendra remembered how Steph had once noticed the way her figure made Richard nervous, then taken advantage of it at a middle-school dance. He'd edge away when she came close, as if they were two magnets with like poles facing, so Steph had fun 'pushing' him around the punch bowl.

"No, no it's, um…" Richard started to have trouble knowing what to do with his hands. Kendra felt bad for her friend, so she steered the conversation to the game they'd just played, working out how it might have gone if he really had cast a spell to give her dick legs. Richard figured it was for the best he hadn't, as it would have added a weird layer to when her character kicked the villain in her crotch. Their laughter warmed them against the falling temperature.

They stopped at the t-junction where they'd have to part ways.

"Okay," Richard said, "see you on Monday, I guess."

"See you then!"

They'd only gone a dozen paces in opposite directions when

Kendra felt a tension in her chest and stopped. Turning, she ran up to Richard, seizing his hand.

"Richard?"

"Y-yes?"

"Have you seen my dog? I really miss him."

XOXO

By Sunday morning Kendra couldn't wait any longer. The previous evening, she and her dad had walked around the neighborhood to no avail. She needed to do more, to not feel as powerless as she had for the past few days. So there Kendra sat at the family desktop computer, in the space where dining and living room met, full of blueberry pancakes and frustration. Her father's pirated copy of Photoshop didn't always behave and she was having trouble getting the cursor to settle where she needed it to finish her simple, black and white poster to put up around the neighborhood. Getting a job and earning the money for her own computer would have to become a priority, especially since she'd 'spent' Christmas and her birthday on those headphones.

"Dad! This thing is bullshit!" she called across the house, "Help!"

"Don't swear, please!" he called back, approaching his daughter from the other end of their home.

"Greg swears all the time." Kendra replied as her father settled behind her, resting one thickly thatched hand on her shoulder.

"Yeah and he gets in trouble for it all the time. Plus, he's gross."

Kendra laughed, then paid close attention as her father helped her finish the poster. She cared about being be able to do things like this herself. When the printer kicked into gear, she reached over to give him a hug and was treated to a deep inhalation of the unique odor her father had. Dad-smell was hard to quantify and Kendra never really wanted to break it down, not wanting to demystify him in any way.

Thirty copies of her poster in hand, Kendra trailed behind her father as he headed back to the parental bedroom and she headed to her own, for a folder or maybe a binder clip. Hearing something interesting as she came alongside her brother's door, Kendra paused and listened closely.

"Fuck, I mean, it's so unfair." Greg said, "Like, all a girl has to do to get laid is stand on the porch and ring a dinner bell."

That was everything Kendra heard before the posters slipped from her fingers to the carpet. Three copies slid directly under her brother's door. Scrabbling for the few dozen two-dimensional Salvador Doggies on the floor, Kendra only saw Greg's feet as he appeared, kicking the couple of posters in his room back out to her.

"Screw off, you little spy!"

Red-faced, she said nothing, wincing as the door was slammed in her ear.

A minute later, Kendra stood on the front steps of the house with an elastic band stretched around the posters and a bulky, heather grey sweater tossed on over her faded black, science museum t-shirt. Boyfriend jeans kept all but her ankles warm, summer socks reaching up from doughy white sneakers to compensate. While her and her father had been looking around for Salvador the previous day, he'd kept insisting various boys were checking her out. At first she was embarrassed and then she'd become irritated, even though she knew he meant well. He always seemed to be doing that, probably trying not to be like those weird Dads in shows and movies who worked so hard to keep boys away from their daughters, as if they were trying to protect their stock from cattle thieves. Her Mom once said he was only trying to open her eyes a little; Kendra didn't buy it.

Figuring out where the imagery in Greg's complaint came from wasn't difficult. The family had an antique dinner bell hanging above their porch, a relic from her great-great-grandfather's farm that had fallen victim to the brutal dust storms of April 14th, 1935 - "Black Sunday". Though it was lost to her and her parents generation, Kendra's grandfather on her mother's side still had a bit of an Oklahoma twang when he spoke. Sometimes she liked to imagine being a prairie farmer. Today Kendra just wondered what was wrong with whatever her 'dinner bell' was, then decided to imagine Salvador's little face instead. Smiling, hair set free of a few clips, she stepped out onto the narrow streets of the old suburb she called home.

1970's brick and aluminum bungalows, some two stories tall but never three, with short laneways and wide front lawns. Tall metal lamp posts planted in speckled concrete bases, many of which had small chips taken out of them by careless drivers over the years. Homes organized in long, rectangular blocks lacking any of the crescents which would come into fashion later in the twentieth century. Not a heck of a lot of places for Kendra to put up posters, so she planned a route to pass the greatest number of lamp posts and public mail boxes possible while taking her towards the nearest strip mall.

A roll of duct tape scavenged from the bottom kitchen drawer completed her kit and she fought to get it started, her nails kept short with weekly clippings. Maybe more boys would notice her if she grew them longer and got into painting the damn things? Images of constellations painted on dark blue nails had barely swirled into focus when Kevin jogged his way into her vision, the soft thup-thup-thup of sneakers heralding his arrival just before he passed the last length of a tall ceder hedge. Kendra feigned an even greater interest in her tape problem as if she, standing on an otherwise empty roadside, might somehow vanish. Too late, here he came, swinging that stuff of his within a pair of blue soccer shorts.

"Hey Kendra!"

"Oh…hey Kevin." She took her time looking up from the tape, fingers still picking away even as their eyes met, "So, did you and Mary totally get it on or what?"

"What? No." He didn't seem to catch the friendliness woven into Kendra's tease, "We just ran for a while. She mumbled something about sunflowers being the best flower because you can look them in the eye."

"Ha! What a weirdo."

"Yeah, I guess so."

Damn, she'd been looking *him* in the eye, those green eyes of his, for too long. Kendra glanced behind and down the street as if to check for a bus. A brainstorm came instead.

"I guess you're jogging, but can you help me with something?"

"Uh, maybe. What?" Her fingers ran back along his as she handed him the roll of tape.

"First I'd love it if you could get this dumb roll of tape started." Hands now free, the posters under one arm, she quickly performed some hair clip maintenance, "Then I was thinking, would you help me put up these posters? My dog is missing."

Putting her hair back the way she liked it, Kendra held up a poster for Kevin. Reading Salvador's name, he let out a short laugh that went a long way with the dog's owner. Kendra exaggerated, desperate to make sure he'd be sympathetic enough to want to help, and told him Salvador had been missing for two weeks. It worked.

They began walking together. There was rarely a place where they could both be putting up posters at the same time, so Kendra often struggled to make a single poster into a two person task, having Kevin hold the paper in place while the she taped. Mostly Kevin was company for her, which was just what she wanted. He didn't say much, he didn't have to.

With about a third of the posters put up, they came to the back parking lot of the nearest strip mall. Kids a little bit older than them gathered here to be aggressively bored in the way you do when your neighborhood offers little else to do than eating or shopping. Kendra was glad those kids would never be there around noon on a Sunday; she was afraid of earning their attention and getting teased. Having caught an awful lot of that kind of heat in grade school, she hoped to transcend to a better way of life in high school. It wasn't happening as quickly as she liked, any progress made possible not by her shining brighter but by there being a couple of people even further down the totem pole.

"So, Mary wanted you to come see some sunflowers? That's kinda..."

"Well, I guess it coulda been nice for, like, a minute." Kevin added. His interest in helping seemed to be dripping away. Kendra was grateful when her stomach growled.

"Hey, how about we take a break and get some food? Maybe Subway?" He answered her with a bobbing nod. Jesus he seemed relaxed, couldn't he feel the tension here? Whatever, she was doing okay, she was doing okay.

Kendra thought of the time her parents had taken her and her brother to a Hershey chocolate factory, how the smell had hit them the second they stepped out of the car, and how that smell was so much more pleasant than the massive bread fart fighting up her nose as she and Kevin entered the Subway. Passing through the door, she imagined Golems made of Subway bread hunting children through the woods, the only warning being the waft of their odor passing along icy Germanic winds, between tall, dark conifers and into the nostrils of lederhosen clad, chubby-cheeked blonds. Maybe the smell would contain spores who'd embed themselves in the children's cell walls, eventually reaching critical mass and transforming the children into fresh Subway Golems? Subway Fresh (tm) Bread Golems.

"So, what can I get you today?"

Kendra tried to make small talk as they crab-shuffled towards the cash, only making it take longer for them to sort out the toppings on their sandwiches when the server interrupted. Annoyed, Kendra clamped her mouth shut until they were seated opposite each other, a little too close to speakers pumping out the contents of a corporate sanctioned, pop music playlist. Was this a date now? Was this her first date? She wished she could get away with texting Val or Gwen to consult them. Her only option now was to use what she knew.

"So Kevin, want to hear something cool?"

"Sure."

Gah, why did she take such a big bite while he answered? It felt like a timer had started and if it ran out before she finished forcing down a wad of bread, cheese, onions, and most of two meatballs then he'd vanish. She shrugged at him, one cheek looking like she'd hid a tennis ball in there, rolling her eyes at herself in a way he'd hopefully find funny. Eventually a hard swallow came, the timer having not quite run out.

Kendra decided to try sharing something interesting she'd read about lately, the Finnish Baby Box program. Kevin thought you only put a baby in a box if you wanted to leave it on someone's doorstep, so Kendra went on in great detail about how new parents in Finland are sent a box with a kit of starter supplies inside, with the idea being that the box is then used as the baby's first crib. This had been going on since the 1930's, meaning almost everyone in Finland had been a baby in a box at one point.

Kevin chewed, nodding his head side to side in thought. She

noticed he was eating his cookies first. Interesting. Maybe she should look up a Youtube tutorial on how to make them?

"Okay, sure. Maybe it's cuz I'm a guy, but I don't think much about babies. Probably won't for a while, too."

Kendra imagined saying he probably thought more about how they're made and felt her meatball-stuffed cheeks - why did she keep taking such huge bites? - grow warm at the idea. Instead, once she swallowed, Kendra decided to try something she was more comfortable discussing.

"Uhm, what are you reading right now? I'm reading the Clan of The Cave Bear books. Well, the 'Earth's Children' series, I think they're really called. They're all about this Cro-Magnon cave girl growing up with Neanderthals and she even has a kid with one? No baby box for her. The first book is pretty decent, but the second one..." Her face grew flush again, "...it's, it's really good."

"Cool. I don't really read books, though."

"What?" Kendra couldn't process this at first. Her parents had taken turns reading to her from before she could remember, stopping only when she kept reading over their shoulders because the story wasn't coming fast enough for her liking, "Didn't your parents read to you?"

"When I was little, I guess. They didn't make a big deal about it."

Kendra wondered if it was too late to call child services on them. Struggling to rally from this, she had to sip her soda and think for a second before remembering Kevin was in her English class.

"But you read for school, right? How else are you gonna write a paper on Lord of the Flies?"

"Yeah." He sniffed, "It's actually pretty badass. I think I'm going to write my essay about how awesome it is they don't have any parents around."

"For sure! I mean, I think I'm pretty lucky, but parents are still parents." She smiled, glad to have found the ultimate common denominator, bitching about your folks, "My Mom has to work all kinds of weird hours and she gets crazy cranky some days."

"What's she do?" Kevin was almost done his meal. Kendra could only milk her soda and cookies so long, then she'd be stuck trying to keep him convinced postering was a two person job again. She tapped her fingers against the waxy paper of her cup.

"Oh she's, like, a firewoman? Fireman? Fireperson?" Kendra jumped a little in her seat as Kevin gave the table a hearty slap.

"That's awesome! That's so awesome. She must have all kinds of amazing stories."

"Uh, some? She's usually too tired and I think some stories, well, some stories she doesn't really want to share."

"Like a war hero, cool." He scrunched up his garbage and tossed it away, not recycling. Normally she'd care, but… "God, that's so much better than my parents. You know, in a way it kind of sucks there weren't any parents on the island."

"In the book?" Kendra reluctantly stood up and saw to her own recycling.

"Yeah. Like, just one set of parents, Piggy's maybe." They

headed for the door.

"Maybe! But the whole book is about how they change away from their parents, so, like..." A tightly wound spring pulled the door shut behind Kevin so sharply it nearly hit Kendra in the nose.

"Sorry, what?" She said, squinting a little and stepping outside.

"I said." Kevin stood arms akimbo, facing away from her, toward the much larger front parking lot, "They could kill them."

"Whoah, that'd be nuts."

"I mean," Still looking away, "I just want to kill my dad sometimes, you know?"

"Oh I hear you. One time, my mom-"

"He's just so shitty." Kevin wasn't listening, "Sometimes I see him working under our car and I want to kick the jack out so it falls and crushes his stupid head."

Kendra laughed nervously, not sure what to make of the strain that had appeared in Kevin's voice. Turning to her left, she wondered what the hell was going on at this guy's home and what it meant for their date. Kevin had gone quiet and she hoped it meant he'd calmed down.

She saw him finish walking over a dozen feet away from her, along the storefronts, to feign interest in a shoe shining machine on display at the barber's. A familiar energy shot through her body and Kendra turned her head with perfect accuracy, spotting a cluster of confident, stylish girls walking by the other end of the parking lot. They were looking in Kevin's direction and he seemed to be trying to find the courage to look back. Mouth set in a subtle frown, she leaned against the Subway's glass storefront, not caring that her butt was level with someone's lunch. She stayed there until Kevin was done checking out that really cool shoe shine machine, which happened to be about two seconds after the other girls exited the scene.

They left to put up a few more posters over the course of a mostly quiet hour, exchanging just the basic sentences required for postering. Kendra's desire for Kevin slowly desaturated, surprising her, as the truth of their incompatibility became harder and harder to ignore. Why couldn't they just go find a quiet, private place in the park and run their hands all over each other? Wasn't casual sex a thing in the world? Wasn't liking someone's body even if you didn't like their personality a thing? There were jokes about guys being like that all the time. Maybe those jokes weren't so fair or true. Gah. Each time they did another poster it became clearer Kevin was trying to work up the courage to beg off.

"It's okay Kevin, you've helped enough today. Thanks."

He nearly thanked her back, for being released. His mouth only opened a crack before closing again, moving up and down with the rest of his face as he gave another one of those bobbing nods she no longer thought was cute. Behind her, Kevin thup-thup-thupped into the distance. It would have been nice to have touched him more, at least. To be touched. To be seen, truly seen by him. For a car to fall on his stupid head. Okay, not really. Ugh. Could her feelings maybe be a little more consistent, please?

Feeling her body giving a cold weather alert, Kendra was glad she hadn't worn the form-fitting pearl blue turtleneck her grandmother had given her last year. Crossing her arms anyways, she thought over how this wasn't something boys really worried about, even though she'd read that a lot of guys get erect nipples when they're aroused. In middle-school there'd been the notorious minority known as The Binder Boys, those special guys who had so much trouble with involuntary erections they had to resort to a pretty unsubtle use of their school materials to cover up their embarrassment, sometimes while walking the halls. Turning a corner, Kendra wondered about a world where cold weather gave men silly, swinging erections and bent over laughing so hard she ran out of breath. Running with the imagery, imagining table lamps and dinner plates being sent to shatter on cold kitchen floors while twirling men apologized in absurdly deep voices, kept her in that position.

Looking up, her laughter-smile was kept in place by a welcome sight. Twenty feet ahead was a familiar four-legged waddle. She couldn't tell where Salvador Doggy had come from, exactly, but she didn't care. Kendra ran forward and scooped up his dense brown mass, closing her eyes just before Salvador's tongue ran over them. She pinched the back of his neck with her teeth. Salvador licked his lips and yawned, his owner's skinny arms struggling to hold him as high as possible, a prize for all to see in the comforting light of a Fall sun.

"Mine!" Kendra cried out, "Always mine, forever and ever and fuck you too!"

Swaddling him within her sweater, hard little paws pressed

against her chest, Kendra ran homeward. Their eyes and mouths were open wide with delight, catching the kinds of gently blowing breezes that, felt again years from now, would conjure the memory of this moment.

A few weeks later, Val and Kendra lay sprawled across the two old couches in the latter's living room. Val was listening to her friend dissect, for at least the third time, every glance and comment composing the story of postering with Kevin. She sympathized, said that hey, she hadn't had sex yet either, and she'd also had a kind-of-date that didn't lead anywhere. As Kendra began a "No, but…" to try and establish who'd found fewer rewards in the badlands of boys, her mother interrupted to let them know she'd just had a call from a neighbor one block over. This neighbor, owner of the only other dachshund in the neighborhood, was letting them know Salvador had gotten their dog, Barkwurst, pregnant. Her mom made a not-so-whispered aside to her dad, asking if they'd need to explain "How the sausage-dog is made" and Val laughed. Delight at the prospect of puppies was put on hold, as Kendra turned from her mother to ponder an animal for whom sex was so much simpler, an animal who was happily wolfing down some dry food he'd scattered out of his bowl.

"Nrrrrryam yam yam." Salvador said, lapping up little brown x's and o's, "Nyam nam nam."

PART TWO

Level Out

It was the first weekend of Grade Eleven. Kendra sat in Gwen's bedroom, her friend fetching drinks in the kitchen. Everything looked so different from the way it was during her last visit which, truth be told, had been over a year ago. The summer vacation just past, Gwen's family had gone on a six-week trip across America and the other couple of weeks Gwen had been knocked out with mono. All of which had suited Kendra just fine, really, since Grade Ten had been a year of their friendship steadily melting away. Gwen was getting more interested in drama class, her new drama friends, and telling everyone around her how to handle their personal dramas. This took up a lot of her time, and she was never in any rush to mix friend groups, so Val and Kendra had been shoved to the margins.

Well, just Kendra these days - ever since Gwen tried to tell Val how she could benefit from mummifying her torso and thighs in plastic wrap, then laying under a heat lamp for an hour before a date. Being told, unsolicited, you should sweat out a few pounds so you can look a little thinner is not always the greatest mood enhancer and Val told Gwen this in no uncertain terms. A few snippy remarks were exchanged before Val and Gwen had stormed off in opposite directions, leaving Kendra at her locker to slide down onto the floor, hiding behind a second-hand copy of Marian Engel's "Bear". Kendra hated thinking of that awkward scene so much, she was having trouble remembering how she'd navigated the fallout from her not having followed either them.

Most of Grade Ten was difficult to remember. It stunned Kendra how few new experiences or adventures she'd had that year. There hadn't even been any notable encounters with bullies. The one boy she'd liked, Scott Allison, had been a long stretch of unrequited longing and research. Not wanting to be surprised by any strangeness, like Kevin's parental issues, she'd done everything she could online and offline to learn about him. Presented with the opportunity one day, she'd even taken a quick sniff of his gym clothes; a test he'd passed so well she'd nearly embarrassed herself trying for a second sniff the next day. Eventually Kendra had joined the school improv club as a way to be around him. She made sure they chatted for at least a few minutes at every weekly meeting, Thursday's at lunch, for almost the entire school year. As Summer vacation approached and Kendra still hadn't found the courage to ask him out. Then came the final improv meet of the year; she knew she had to act.

She'd overheard him telling a different member of the troupe his older sister was worried she might be pregnant. Leaping into the conversation, Kendra had said "Oh man, was it that Azad guy she met when she was doing her marketing co-op?" and he'd been stunned she remembered that level of detail from what the two of them had chatted about over the year.

"Oh I remember, like, everything you've told me!" she'd said, so sure this would impress him. Kendra had gone on, with plenty of excited hand motions, to regurgitate facts about Scott's family, this weird dream he'd had three months ago, the story of a fight he nearly got into behind the gym, his middle-school girlfriend, why he always liked to try and work squirrels into a sketch when he was on stage in improv…

Throat starting to go sore from twenty minutes or so of pouring her memory banks all over Scott - and not picking up on his total silence - she asked him what he remembered about her.

"Uh." He'd mumbled, "I think you've got, like, a sister?"

That was the last time Kendra went to improv.

Meanwhile, she was still trying to process the changes in Gwen's room. Gone was her friend's copy of the trophy they'd won playing doubles at tennis camp, the large poster of a giraffe had been replaced by a reprint of the poster for a 1950's production of "Guys and Dolls", and the walls had turned from golden yellow to pale grey. Just before Gwen came back in, a glass of iced tea in each hand, Kendra spotted two books she'd lent Gwen halfway through Grade Nine. Neither Margaret Atwood's "Oryx and Crake" nor Ursula K. Leguin's "The Left Hand of Darkness" seemed to have seen any action, their bookmarks still sitting right where Kendra had left them.

"Okay, so I thought about it in the kitchen and I know what you need to do." Gwen handed over a glass with a little too much powder at the bottom, she never was thorough enough when stirring the mix for these, "But you may not like it. Can you promise not to get mad, like Val always does?"

Like Val did just one time. Kendra thought before replying, "Sure, no problem. I promise not to get mad." Gwen settled on the end of her bed, not beside her on the floor.

"So okay, we could get into clothes. I mean, you still kind of dress like you did in middle school, but I don't think that's really the thing." A sip, "We could talk about how you think it's attractive to talk about weird sex facts with boys, but I don't think that's the thing either. Not the most important thing, anyway."

Kendra looked down into her glass. Between Kevin and Scott there had been this boy with a hazel brown fringe she and Gwen got talking to at a birthday party for one of Gwen's new theater pals. He'd been telling them both about his trip to a Ripley's Believe It or Not and all the weird stuff he saw there, especially the records of human oddities. Figuring it'd be in his wheelhouse, Kendra had brought up the Icelandic Penis Museum.

"Well, the Phallological Museum." She'd said, before telling what she thought was the very compelling story of the owner's quest to bring a human member into his collection. She thought the American who wanted to donate his penis, who sent photos of it dressed up like Santa Claus and Abraham Lincoln, was a great story. She even offered to link the boy to where he could torrent a Canadian documentary about the museum. He simply said "No", in that way which says a person has just formed a very simple, very negative opinion of the speaker. Then he walked off. Gwen didn't exactly have her back on that one. Jesus, why was she still friends with her?

Momentum, mostly. Gwen was her first female friend, having met both her and Paul on the first day of pre-school. Kendra had never gone through any kind of Boys Are Gross phase when she was little. Sometimes, remembering the conversation her brother's friends had had about her body two years ago, she thought she might go into that phase now. It'd have to be a selective declaration of grossness, though, since she'd just spotted this one guy who-

"Kendra, are you listening?"

"Yeah." Sip, "Shut up."

Kendra leaned back against the wall, away from the sunlight coming in through the window and into the shadow beneath the frame. Gwen had always liked figuring things out. They'd first bonded over solving the problem of how to keep worms alive when bringing them home from the playground. Now she just wanted to 'figure out' people's bodies and social lives, whether or not she was asked.

"For you to get laid, you need to look at someone on your level." Gwen continued.

"My level?"

"Yeah." She smiled, "It's like, a penguin doesn't get too far if it tries to sleep with a lion, and it never will. However, if it focuses on penguins…"

"And my fellow penguins are?" Kendra squinted, ignoring the strange choice of metaphor, feeling the start of an intangible swirling somewhere between her chest and her stomach.

"Well, they're not guys like Kevin or Jay - the guy from the party you weirded out." Gwen got down on the carpet and sat opposite Kendra because oh gosh they sure were connecting now, "Scott was a good idea, but I guess that didn't play. Then again, he's pretty good looking for an Improv kid."

Oh yes, they were really connecting now. Each one was present both in the room and in their own personal fantasy involving the other. Gwen's was likely about her jump-starting Kendra's non-existent love life and all the other girls who, after seeing her success with this skinny nerd who didn't even know how to use make-up, would seek out her wisdom. Kendra's fantasy involving Gwen began as a simple red dot of frustration that was blossoming into something like the bucket of pig blood scene in Carrie. Of course, in that scenario Kendra would likely be the one getting the bucket dumped on her and-

"Oh my god, screw this." Kendra stood up fast, bumping her shoulder against the window frame. She'd gone from 5'4 to 5'8 over the summer and still wasn't used to her new proportions, "I gotta go, I have a homework to do."

"A homework?"

"Yeah." Kendra took a careful step around Gwen, "Singular. One unit of homework. A cluster of homeworks is called a 'Boredom', as in 'a boredom of homeworks', just FYI."

"Kendra." Gwen stood up as well, like a ballerina going back to first position, "I'm serious, you chase the wrong boys. You should ask out one of those guys you do role-playing games with. I think Richard has the least going against him."

"Oh my god." Kendra spun around to look Gwen in the eye, "Gwen, those are my friends!"

"Come on, you know Richard would probably-"

“And you aren’t! Not anymore!” Kendra snatched her books and made a clumsy attempt at slamming Gwen’s bedroom door behind her, denied a cathartic impact by the humidity-swollen wood dragging along the carpet. Gratefully, Gwen’s parents were in the back yard so nobody had to see her stumble and drop her books as she did the one foot hop while rushing to get her shoes on. She’d had her shaky, angry moment and didn’t want Gwen adding another scene on the end of their friendship with some sort of cloakroom confrontation. Gwen didn’t come out before she left, though, she didn’t even look out her window to watch Kendra stomp across wet leaves toward the bus stop by the soccer field.

Sitting on the number ninety-seven, Kendra held a hand to her temple and ran her tongue over dry, cracked lips. Gwen’s condescending advice was one more strand of annoyance, slipping through to intertwine with a host of others, binding them all into a painful Gordian knot right behind her forehead. The pattern on the seat in front of her, a prismatic spray of geometric outlines spread across an inky blue ocean, did little to relax her. Texting Val the details, she read her friend’s righteous and sympathetic indignation; it helped a little bit. Kendra continued to calm down once she was home, ensconced in her room, laying back in bed with her new, powerful tablet. She’d bought it using money from a part-time job at the same damn Subway she’d visited with Kevin.

Kendra had gleefully quit just before the school year began, scorching earth by lying about her father having gotten a job offer in Australia and how they were moving there immediately so no she couldn't work a few more shifts to help bridge the gap from her to whomever the new hire would be. Springing the same wry smile she'd worn while leaving her skeptical manager alone in his tiny office, Kendra opened her copy of Photoshop and snatched a few pictures of cute boys from Facebook. Halfway through sticking their heads on some gay porn she'd whistled up, there was a scratching at her bedroom door. The scratching grew more impassioned and was soon joined by a few howls.

"Kendra, see what the dogs want!" Her mother called from down the hallway. They'd taken on two of Salvador's love children, Honey Garlic & Spicy Italian. Greg's laziness meant they were almost exclusively Kendra's responsibility. She didn't mind, most days.

"Kendra, come on, it's not fair to make them wait for food!"

Kendra was tempted to tell her mother to do it, but she knew she was trying to rest up for an overnight shift at the station. Irritated by how slowly the embarrassing windows on her tablet were closing, she just shoved it under her mattress. After catching her brother saving porn on the family computer in a folder he'd labeled 'Dinosaur Pictures', she knew he was out to get her back.

The dogs got even more excited when Kendra, in her haste to leap off her bed, forgot about the junk she'd left on the end. Her right foot couldn't have connected better if she tried, sending her trusty plastic container of thirty-six dice flying into the door to crack open and spill its contents everywhere. Sighing, she crouched down to begin scooping them up. Checking the results, she saw over half of the dice had come up a six.

"Huh, hope I roll that well tomorrow."

Level Up

At the next day's lunch period, Kendra's hand wasn't giving her the same payoff her foot had. Paul, Richard, Tim, and Kendra were playing Wizard Bastards, a collectible dice based game that could be won or lost in fifteen minutes. Each semi-transparent, candy-colored die had an array of symbols on them representing various spells wielded by each of the competing wizards/players. RPGs were too long for the lunch hour and the sight of her and the guys acting out their character's actions drew the wrong kind of attention from various subgenuses of jerk.

This worked out well, except Tim kept throwing too hard, sending his dice outside their circle to skitter off toward the nearest girl's washroom. Tim also couldn't help shaking his dice in a motion almost identical to jerking off. While he went chasing after his dice, Kendra commented "Geez, I hope dice are the only thing he keeps spilling all over the floor like that."

Her throat a little dry, she'd spoken at a volume only Richard heard. He grinned, then repeated exactly what Kendra had said. Paul laughed long and hard at this, going so far as to slap one of his knobby knees. Richard joined him, reacting much more enthusiastically than he had to Kendra.

"I just said that!" Kendra pointed at Richard, "I just made the same joke and then you repeated it."

"What joke?" Tim had returned. Paul gave the joke thief a snotty look. Richard just shrugged.

"Yeah, what joke?", Val had come over behind Kendra, who swept up some bright red dice and stood to meet her, "I got an extension on my English paper, so I don't have to finish before lunch is over. I can help you with whatever it is you needed help with."

"Great. Grab your jacket." Kendra opened her locker to pull out her own jacket, a white denim affair she'd thought was cool in the store and regretted ever since she'd recycled the receipt, "Sorry guys, I'm out for now."

Walking away from school with Val, Kendra began to fume as she thought back to the pals she'd just left to keep playing Wizard Bastards. They'd all been friends for ages and had always enjoyed a camaraderie built from shared interests combined with unity in the face of bullies. She resented Gwen for her idea that she should sleep with one of them because they were on 'her level'; for forcing her to look at them that way. She resented herself for finding them lacking in attractiveness and social skills, for giving into the very idea of cliques and levels and whatever by disliking being grouped with them even when they were among her best, most dependable friends. Meanwhile, she'd failed to have sex before turning sixteen and Gwen was probably forgetting what being a virgin even felt like.

Fine, whatever, Kendra thought, *Sixteen is pretty much the national average so long as I do it before I turn seventeen then I'm good.*

All this frustration was funneled into a one woman comedy roast of her clothing and general appearance. Val alternated between sympathetic laughter and solemn nodding.

"So okay, you want me to help you find some new clothes. Where do you want to go?" She asked, when Kendra paused to breath.

After buying her high-end tablet, Kendra knew she'd not be able to afford more than a few pairs of socks unless they went to a nearby Goodwill.

As they entered, a blue-aproned cashier began admiring Val's pixie cut. Kendra had helped her get it just right, so she wasn't sure whether to be proud or jealous. As so often happened, she was treated to a sweetly acidic mixture of two feelings. Sometimes it was hard watching Val get all the attention she did, attention Val never seemed to notice; this was compensated for by the strength of their friendship and, frankly, the continued fact of Val being stuck on the deck of the S.S. Virgin right there with her. More than the solidarity with her gaming pals against bullies, this helped keep Kendra sane in the face of High School and all that came with it.

"How about this?" Val called out, lifting a red sun dress with ruffles along the bottom.

"How about this?" Kendra held up a pair of donated men's briefs some brave soul had hung up with a dress pants hanger, "More like tighty *off*-whitey's, right?"

Up and down the racks they went, sifting through threadbare

jeans, clothing by large labels who had stopped being fashionable when the two girls were still learning the names of basic shapes, and faded polo shirts with rumpled collars. One of those shirts set more kindling on the fire in Kendra's belly, a red polo not unlike one she had on under her white denim. It even had a logo from a local business, some plumbing outfit, much as her shirt had a golden stitched logo from her father's work.

Thrusting this back on the rack, Kendra closed her eyes and thought hard. She wanted something different, cool, and sexy. She also wanted something to make her feel stronger, and shielded against whatever the world might throw at her. Something to give her the confidence to, if not transcend her 'level' or whatever, move on to a more assertive and exciting daily existence. Opening her eyes, Kendra didn't know what that was.

Then an old man accidentally crashed his shopping cart into a rack way over on the other side of the store. Looking toward the noise, Kendra had the kind of feeling she couldn't stop to asses or debate. Instead, she rode it over to the rack he'd collided with and assembled her armor, images of Pam Grier in Jackie Brown, Janelle Monáe in one of her early videos, and, of course, Dianne Keaton in Annie Hall flowing through her mind.

Standing in the changing room, she shed the red polo, the boyfriend jeans, and the umpteenth pair of puffy white sneakers in her life. Wondering about the thin crack in the changing room's door and where that old man might be, she got dressed. The clothes not being tailored for her, she had to do some careful tucking in, rolling up of pants legs, and several shiftings of shoulders before feeling comfortable. So okay, this was it, this was definitely it.

What Val saw step out of the changing room was someone doing their best to replace grey areas and fuzzy definitions with sharp lines and clear contrasts; Skinny black tie, bright white men's dress shirt, black suit jacket, black dress pants. White sneakers and chunky, beige frames would have to stay until Kendra could beg her parents for some new, slender, circular black frames and a pair of black converse sneakers to finish the look.

"A whole suit for thirty dollars, right?" Kendra tried to pose, got impatient and did a couple of quick jumping jacks to burn the energy racing around her body, pearly teeth shining from behind cracked lips. Val came over with grape-flavor balm and set about applying it to her friend before something started bleeding.

"Kendra Grape-Flavor Washington, you look great."

"I don't have a middle name, and if I did it wouldn't be Grape-Flavor."

"But what if it was?" Val replied.

Returning to school, she did indeed get a lot of attention. Paul nodded his approval, Richard scratched the back of his head, and Tim seemed to be trying to stroke a beard he couldn't grow yet. Others mostly stared, then made comments to each other; not all negative. A jerk from the year ahead of Kendra, however, had to ask "Uh, isn't that a suit?"

"It seems so, doesn't it?" Kendra replied, full of cheer. With each step forward, each swing of an arm, she relished the feel of the fabric's desire to shoot along her limbs. Remembering nineteenth century tycoons from a book of old political cartoons, Kendra put her hands on each of her jacket's lapels and tugged at them whenever she met someone's gaze. Her tower of hair was top hat enough.

Kendra had already made up her mind that this was it, this was the direction she wanted to go in her escape from the middle-school cocoon of comfort-focused clothing she'd felt hampered by since long before Gwen opened her stupid mouth about anything. Yet it didn't hurt when she caught an admiring look, maybe the first one she'd ever noticed, directed her way from the deep green eyes of the one guy she could never include in a late-blooming Boys Are Gross phase, were she ever to enter one.

William Daniels.

Cooler

Mr. Gregory drew everyone's attention to the board, trying to impart one final piece of wisdom before World Issues class ended. Kendra eyes were aimed at her notes about increasing instability in West Africa but she wasn't seeing them; her skin was a little flush, her legs a little crossed, her mind more than a little focused on absorbing every detail of what had interrupted her running track that morning.

Paying no attention to Mary or Kevin whenever they lapped her, Kendra glanced into the woods surrounding half the schoolyard and most of the track. Flickers of movement between the trees caught her eye and so, breaking from the loops of white chalk, she jogged over to the nearest fir and poked her head around the side. Seeing more flickers, just enough to recognize as people, she felt the sweat under her shirt turn cold. Kendra undid the arms of the navy blue fleece hugging her waist, wriggled into it, and set to exploring.

Stepping between brush, a scattering of cigarette butts and candy wrappers was her first discovery; older kid detritus. Crouching down to poke at this with her index finger, she supposed she was getting to be among the older kids, though she still had until January before turning seventeen. She wanted her Older Kid years to be as interesting and mysterious as those kids had always seemed in the past.

"Well, better find something interesting and mysterious, I guess." Kendra whispered, "Or some way to be interesting and-"

POK

Something hit her.

Looking up, Kendra saw a squirrel on a high branch. He'd just dropped a half-eaten acorn on her head and was chittering away furiously, trying to scare her off so he could clamber down to finish it. His hairy little features were framed by a bold stir of marbled clouds being shaped into mountainous forms by passionate winds, adding such an air of gravitas to his scoldings Kendra couldn't help laughing. Wanting to share this, she pulled out her phone but, just as she got the perfect shot lined up, the camera app crashed. Kendra cursed under her breath. She was sure the parental control program her Mom had put on there, for fear her daughter might see something inappropriate with its web browser, was causing glitchy behavior. She'd have to learn how to do something about that.

Kendra heard what sounded like glass rattling, mixed with a heavy object hitting the bottom of a hole in the earth. Finding their way behind her eyes were visions of some of the more analog dangers her mother wanted to protect her from. Yet, when she stood up and began walking through the woods again, the squirrel watched her go in the direction of the noise, not away.

"Awesome, it fit."

Will Daniels.

“I’ll get some leaves.”

A girl? Kendra wondered, *What fresh bullshit is this?*

She got down on the ground and clambered toward the thickest bush on her side of a small clearing. Will Daniels was standing over by the far side. She couldn’t spy what had been placed in the ground, only the width of the hole as given away by displaced earth - about three feet - and a strong, smooth-skinned hand resting on the haft of a shovel. A sprinkle of freckles had been tossed beneath each of those green eyes of his, resting along cheekbones that would fit so well in her palms. Kendra wished his red hair wasn’t so short, but admired the reason why. It was growing out from, when his father went through chemotherapy, his having shown solidarity with a shorn scalp. The old hunting jacket he wore looked like it would be cozy to just open up, flatten out, and lay in. By a fire. With a freckled chest as her pillow.

Then the girl stepped into view, dumping an armload of red and orange leaves over the hole, forming a cover over the mystery object. They were spread around by a knee-high black boot with bright white lacing all along the sides and thick, three inch heels. Jesus, it was Azealia.

Kohl eyeliner made dark, knowing eyes stand out even more in their frame of long black bangs with evenly spaced, thin streaks of bowling ball blue. Acne free skin surrounded lips painted the same color as the streaks. A neck like a swan’s led down to the large black bow covering, and drawing attention to, her chest. Despite the weather, Azealia was wearing one of several Japanese school girl outfits she’d tailored in the Gothic

Lolita style, adding black lace gloves, a low-hanging belt of fake pearls, and black & white stripped leggings. This was something of a uniform for Azealia and her crowd, a group of snarky smokers whose shared aesthetic seemed to be their singular interest, other than smoke and snark.

For a brief period Azealia had experimented with a white-girl take on Native American head dresses and accessories. The one time they'd ever spoken to each other, Kendra hadn't gotten very far when she'd tried to explain the difference between cultural appropriation and appreciation. Azealia came from a family with a bit of money, her father being head manager of the local Galtmart big box store, and wasn't used to being told she couldn't do something.

"This is going to be so great when we come back here later." Azealia said, staring at the leaves, "Thanks for helping, Will, I know you hate getting up early."

"Of course I'd help, it's important." He replied, playing with her big black bow, "But if you want-"

Will leaned in and whispered something. Kendra squinted, pretending she knew how to read lips.

"Mmm, yeah." Azealia replied, "I've got an idea."

Keeping one hand on his chest, Azealia sent lace covered fingers down to undo a few buttons on Will's coat. Pushing it open, they found their way south as she looked Will in the eyes and grinned. Kendra saw the crotch of his jeans begin to fill out, just before Azealia's hand blocked her view of something she'd never seen outside of screens. Those binder boys of middle school had always been quick with their portable privacy rectangles and, thankfully, her brother was better at hiding his biology than his porn.

Azealia kept both hands in place as Will gave a firm kiss, gently biting her lower lip, while he gripped the back of her black pleated skirt. Like three gas lamps being lit in unison, everyone felt their faces grow flush. A little voice in Kendra's head kept yelling, louder and louder, for her to look down at the ground and sneak away. She kept still, unable to move even if she'd wanted to. Will pulled up the back of Azealia's skirt while she lifted her leg to wrap around his.

Of course she'd be wearing white panties with some chibi Japanese cartoon frog printed all over them. Kendra bet Azealia didn't even know the character's name; which was Keroppi, thank you very much. There he was by the dozen, laughing, smiling, fishing, reading a book, eating birthday cake, doing a handstand…

For a moment Kendra couldn't believe her mind had wandered away from concern about being some kind of pervert to consternation over Azealia's knowledge of a tiny anime frog. Then she couldn't believe the small gasp of delight Azealia sent into the crook of Will's neck as his fingers slid behind and past the elastic of the offending underwear. She really couldn't believe the damn school bell not only went, but could be so easily heard. One didn't have to go far into the woods to feel like they were in another world.

For one slow motion minute, nobody did anything different.

Chuckling, their eyes resting on each other's collarbones, the two untangled themselves and straightened out their clothes.

Will's coat did a better job than any binder, much to the annoyance of his unseen observer. He took Azealia's hand and they strolled in the direction of the school.

Waiting for another minute, Kendra stood up, knocking the dirt off her knees and elbows. She was already so late it didn't matter if she took a second to solve the mystery of the buried object. Walking over to the leaves, Kendra felt a writhing ball of irritations within her start to lash its tentacles out in several directions. She was irritated for having watched, irritated for being irritated with herself for having watched, irritated Will had a girlfriend, and irritated that for all her recent suit-fueled confidence she felt so much less than Will and Azealia; the two of them seeming free of all anxiety, all self-doubt. They were glowing neon in a watercolour world, both coming off as just so much -

Cooler.

They'd buried a large cooler and inside it were a couple dozen beers, the surrounding earth cold enough to keep them palatable, maybe even tasty. Maybe she could even taste one.

Showing up in home room five minutes late, still wearing her running gear and with 330 ml of beer in her belly, Kendra couldn't stop from saying "Look, I'm just late. What, do you want a bedtime story?" when Ms. Rice asked her why she had been so tardy. Way in the back row of the class, Will let out a hearty laugh.

Dance Panic Ninety-Nine

So there Kendra was, sitting in World Issues, replaying the events from earlier that morning over and over again. She was also looking forward to being able to change when the lunch hour began. Sure Ms. Rice had given her detention, but it had been worth it to speak back to a woman who seemed to think the fate of the free world hung in the balance every time she took attendance.

The rest of the school day passed quickly. In detention Kendra, wanting more suits, pondered ways to earn money that didn't involve another job like she'd had at Subway. While Mary was engrossed with animating a crude CGI leopard in Comm Tech class, Kendra and Val stacked a crescent-shaped wall of chairs around her. They were rewarded by Mary getting just the right kind of annoyed - enough to pout and complain to them, to struggle with the chairs, but not enough to go find a teacher. Richard, on the bus, returned her copy of Lovecraft's "At the Mountains of Madness" and he hadn't even done that horrible thing where he dog-eared the pages instead of using a book mark. Not bad, not bad.

Sitting around the dinner table with her father and brother, mom being on shift, Kendra ate her spaghetti in a state of deep thought. As much as what she'd seen that morning made her want to touch and be touched more than ever, she felt she needed to clear her head of this obsession for at least a little while. Her grades had been coasting along on a steady current of C pluses and B minuses for too long and she was starting to worry how this might narrow her options after graduation. She wasn't sure about taking on the kind of debt college could bring her. She also wasn't sure what she wanted to do with her life, so she couldn't discount a higher education just yet. Her mother thought it was mandatory, her father didn't agree.

Greg was living at home, having graduated from high school back in the spring, and was working at Galtmart while trying to get some fickle friends to follow through on promises of getting him a foot in the door with a construction company.

"Any word from Steve about getting you an interview?" her father asked him.

"No." Greg reached for some garlic bread, "I mean, he said he's trying but…"

"Okay. Maybe it's time you tried moving a few eggs out of your one basket." Face and voice brightening, he shifted his attention to Kendra, "And how about you, Ken? Meet any cute boys lately?"

"Ha ha, Dad. No, they were all sentenced to a life of hard labor on a desert island far away." She stirred her noodles around, listening to the sound of their dogs playing in the backyard, "Didn't you hear? It was terrible -"

"I'm still here."

"I said all the *cute* boys, Greg. Anyways, I'm thinking more about what I want to do when I graduate? Like, I could get better marks if I was more interested in any of the subjects. Maybe if they taught something to do with-"

"I think I could get a job with this house painting company over on-" Greg said.

"Maybe if they taught something to do" Kendra repeated, louder and slower, "with sexual health and gender politics?"

"Didn't you do sex ed in grade eight?" her father asked.

"Yeah, but that's not what I mean. I've been reading-"

"Fan fiction about Doctor Who sticking his dick in Sherlock's ear?" Greg guessed.

"Stop interrupting me!"

"Well, I was still talking about the house painting company and -"

"Bullshit! I was in the middle of answering Dad and you were all 'Ba-duh, house painting you guys?'"

Their father regretted stuffing his mouth full just as Greg made the fan fiction remark. Wanting to get between his children before things escalated, he chewed with gusto.

"And you," Greg replied, "were all 'Uh yeah I'd like to learn how to talk about sex even though my vag is like the yeti, in that it is not only terminally hairy, but no man will ever truly be able to claim to have seen it. Gah buhhhhh.'"

"That doesn't even make any sense, although, who cares right? As long as you're making noises with the poorly wiped anus you call a mouth, as long as you're constantly interrupting me -"

"Kendra!" her father paused for a hard swallow, "Don't be so disgusting."

Kendra tried to argue that everyone in the house swore casually, but her Dad pointed out it was her inventiveness and negativity that took things over the line. Scraping the last of her dinner into the garbage, she chose to leave before desert, citing a need to go work on a school project with Val.

Val's house was a short bus ride away, a corner duplex at the base of a tall hill. People first meeting her mother would agree it wasn't hard to see where her two daughters got their figure from. Having grown close to this little family of women, Val's Dad having died not long after conceiving his twin daughters, Kendra would add that it also wasn't hard to see where Val got her patience and kindness. The patience seemed to have missed Val's sister, Natasha, but she was still kind. This, combined with home knit covers on all the furniture and her familiarity with a house she'd been spending time in since she was six, made the Harris household very welcoming indeed. Soon enough she was sitting opposite Val in the living room, each of them enjoying a skinny, black cat in their laps.

"Your brother's such a jerk." Val agreed, having just been told the tale of dinnertime, "But at least you got to use one of your new catch phrases."

"My what?" Kendra reached for a mug of hot chocolate Val's mother had insisted on giving her before vanishing upstairs to let them have some privacy.

"Lately you've been saying stuff like 'Stop interrupting me', 'I just said that', and 'No explanation needed' an awful lot. Also, swearing like a guy - a guy who likes to swear." Val took a pull from her own hot chocolate, smiling as Kendra frowned at her lap cat when its front paws slid down her chest. The cat looked up at her, confused by its failure to find a footing it was used to finding.

"Yeah. I've been reading a lot more about gender stuff lately." Kendra pet the confused cat back into a curled up position, "Long story short, girls are taught to be more polite, meek, submissive and all that. Girl doctors get interrupted while guys are almost always just listened to and…I dunno, there's a lot of details I could get lost in but the gist is it's better to be more assertive and kind of speak like a guy, not because guys are better but because they aren't given all these conversational handicaps girls are."

"Oh, yeah, okay. I think I tuned out when mom mentioned something like that once. You know how it is when your mom just gets talking, telling you how to behave. Besides, she tends to focus more on the physical stuff." Valerie's mother taught self defense courses for women, five nights a week in a small dojo above a downtown print shop, "Hmm. Think we should start on our World Issues project?"

"Maybe. I don't know how much I want to think about Lagos right now, it's kind of depressing." Kendra thought for a second, "Maybe first we can go to your room and play Dance Panic Ninety-Nine?"

Polishing off their beverages and gently shoving their belly-warming felines onto the floor, they ran up the stairs like girls half their age, hurrying past the thick cloud of weed always standing guard at Natasha's door, and into Valerie's room. A year ago Nat had been caught by her mother with half a gram in her coat pockets. Mrs. Harris decided since her own parents had never succeeded in stopping her from doing the same thing in her teens, and it'd be legal for her daughters when they turned twenty-one, she may as well 'legalize' it. So Natasha was allowed to smoke as much pot as she wanted, provided she did it in her room or in their backyard, kept at least a B+ average, and "bought" from her by completing homework or chores. This blew Kendra's mind more than anything she'd ever inhale or ingest.

Val turned on her TV and console system while Kendra pulled the crinkly, rolled-up controller mat out from under her friend's twin-size bed. Familiar theme music came from the speakers, a mix of classic Japanese video game 8-bit music and late nineties hip-hop. Dance Panic Ninety-Nine's male and female mascots, Egon Electric and Erica Elastic, appeared on either side of the options menu, vogueing in place while Val used a short hop and a step on the mat - a Twister looking thing that worked as a wireless controller - to set up a versus match for her and Kendra. After a warm-up round over some Tokyo DJ's remix of Missy Elliot & Da Brat's "Sock It 2 Me", competition began in earnest over the classic version of Puff Daddy & Ma$e's "Mo' Money, Mo' Problems". The game gave them points for stepping on the colored pads in the correct order and rhythm, while the two of them always kept an unofficial second scoreboard for posturing and posing. Val liked to booty pop, while Kendra was fond of sticking her arms out and back; mugging for an imaginary fish-eye lens looking down at her from the ceiling.

After thirty-five minutes, Kendra had won in both points and poses. Letting the options menu music loop in the background, they sat themselves on the floor, side by side with their backs to the bed frame. Cooling down, Kendra looked over at the small folding table in the far corner of the room. On it was a simple sewing kit and a pair of dark blue jeans. Val's hip size didn't match her waist size, so her mom had had to adjust her daughter's new pants since she was twelve. Val took over when she turned fifteen.

Kendra's gaze swung left from the little sewing table and back to the TV, to Erica Elastic. Erica wore knee high boots, latex hot pants, opera gloves up to her elbows, a kind of deep v-neck bandeau cutting off just under her bust, and a bandanna which seemed unnecessary since her long, black hair was already tied back in a ponytail. The outfit's color scheme was silver and white, with just a touch of gold outlining the bright red power crystal sitting in the middle of her chest. It wouldn't be as simple as adjusting a pair of jeans, but maybe…

"Hey Val." Kendra said, "Would you help me make an outfit so I can cosplay as Erica Elastic at MediaConsumptionCon in February?"

"Ha!" Val clapped her hands together, "Really? Yes, yes I will totally help you dress like her. Think you'll be cool showing so much skin?"

"Well, I don't have abs or anything but my stomach is flat and she basically has the same figure as me, so sure?" She replied, "The guys'll have to look elsewhere if they want some cleavage, but fuck guys."

"Fuck guys, huh?"

"Well, that too. You know what I mean. I think it'd be fun to really throw myself into the con this year. I don't know how many more I'll go to after we finish high school. I mean, you grow out of this shit pretty fast, I think."

Kendra would go on to attend many, many more such conventions after graduating high school.

The bedroom door bumped open and in slouched Natasha, still carrying a small cloud with her.

"What up, dorks."

"Hey Nat."

"Hey sis."

"So, what's the hot gossip already?" Hands stuffed in the pockets of a large black hoodie, Nat's relaxed body language belied her nature. Kendra knew from experience if she didn't soon supply something entertaining, Val's sister would let out a little grunt, then turn around and vanish into her room again. Of course, the early morning had given her a juicy story to tell and her excitement over being able to relay it to the Harris twins erased any worry about being judged a pervert for having watched Will and Azealia make out. As Kendra launched into her story, Nat pulled a hand from her hoodie to shut the bedroom door, then leaned against it.

"So yeah, I guess I won't be getting with Will. At least I got to try having a beer before first period." Kendra shrugged, having finished her story.

"Do you think they'll notice the missing bottle?" Val asked.

"Probably not. The bottles were all loose and I think they had almost thirty in there."

"Must be some kind of party going on in the woods tonight." Val said.

"Maybe it's a going away party." Nat suggested.

"What? For who?" Kendra pushed against the floor to sit up straighter.

"Didn't you hear?" Nat said, "Azealia's dad's being moved to a Galtmart in some dinky little town way out of state. I think it's called Greenville. He's taking the whole family there on Monday."

Fiery Doritos Locos Supreme and a Large Coke

"Okay, I've made up my mind. I'm gonna see if I can make Will like me." Kendra told her friend, the two girls strolling around the schoolyard and wishing either of them had access to a car, "I'll wait a while, though. I'm not a bitch, I mean, a jerk."

"Yes, but Kendra, is he on your level?" Val imitated Gwen's favorite hands-on-hips posture, then threw in a jerk-off gesture for good measure.

"I don't give a shit. Maybe sometimes you want Velma to get with Fred and Shaggy to get with Daphne. But maybe the hell with those two, maybe Shaggy and Velma should just get together and enjoy being way more interesting." Kendra opened her hands like two starbursts going off on either side of her face, "Or maybe the four of them could try meeting some new people who aren't, like, creepy perv-o-sexuals in cheap Halloween costumes?"

"Maybe. Plus a lot of guys dig on Velma. I mean, have you ever Googled 'Sexy Velma photo shoot'?" Val caught the beginning of a curious look coming from Kendra, then glanced down at her feet, "So yeah, like, uh, how long are you going to wait?"

"I think three months from today is good."

A day short of three weeks later, Kendra began to pursue Will. Not having had the best results injecting sex into a relationship through lust-laced trivia, she tried using her body. This led to feeling gross and self-conscious, with Will left curious as to why Kendra was bending over to pick up things she kept dropping around his desk. One time she lost her balance, stumbled forward and drove her face directly into Val's butt, causing her friend to make a noise like a startled parrot. Will's friendly laugh, and the touch of his hands as he helped pick her up off the floor, gave Kendra a better idea.

Seeing Will stuck behind a slow moving cluster of tiny Grade Nines, she mined more laughter by letting him know he was being "walk-blocked". Later, sitting beside him in English Writing, a classmate was reading a terrible poem where every single stanza ended with 'I think I just grew up'. She got a smile by passing him a note with 'I think I just grew up in my mouth' carefully printed in blue pen. It was even better when he began to join in, usually as a partner in critiquing Ms. Rice's tasteless, outdated sweaters; what *was* Gangnam Style anyways? One time Ms. Rice even sent them out into the hall for laughing too much, which hardly felt like punishment. There Kendra was able to learn Will had no siblings, he really liked singers with Irish accents, and his old hunting jacket was a hand-me-down from his grandfather on his mother's side. She told him about her brother's poorly hidden 'Dinosaur Pictures' stash, the time Salvador Doggy filled her mother's helmet with barf right before a shift, and how she was thinking about going into international disaster relief; inspired as much by the A- her and Val got on their Lagos project as any desire to help others.

"Or maybe I'd like to be a therapist?" she added, leaving out how she was thinking about sex therapy in particular. It wasn't until a while after their hallway conversation when Will and Kendra would do more than make the odd joke at someone's expense. She lost track of how many times there seemed to be an opportunity to really talk to him, only for a twinge in her chest or a dryness in her mouth to insist she should stay still until he got on that bus, walked around that corner, or started a conversation with someone else that oh my goodness no she couldn't possibly interrupt or ever join in on.

Two weeks later and Kendra was on her own for lunch. Val was home filling every garbage in the house with snotty tissues, and the guys were clustered around Tim's laptop, watching some old Anime she had no interest in; Paul's arguments about the validity of a show where the characters spent upward of three thirty minute episodes threatening to throw the same fireball having been less than persuasive.

Finding some leftovers of her allowance in the right pocket of her suit jacket, Kendra decided to walk the block and a half from school down to the same strip mall where she'd gotten her suit, one of many which defined the area. Wedged between a copy shop and a holistic healing store, Eat More Accardo's was regularly flooded with students during the lunch hour. Soon Kendra stood at the head of the line, eying up a slice of meat lovers pizza, and was already plotting an exit route through the crowd. She didn't feel like eating alone in the restaurant, especially with Gwen sitting at a table packed with her new theater friends.

Opening her home-made duct tape wallet so she could pay, she tried to remove her student ID to get the discount. Kendra wished she'd taken less of a 'just kinda eyeball it, cut once' approach to making her creation. There were some small patches of exposed stickiness inside, mostly within the folds of her ambitious card divider slots, and one of these made removing her ID almost as much of a project as the wallet had been. When she managed to free her card, it wasn't alone.

"Oh wow!" Gwen shouted, pointing toward the floor "Kendra, did a CONDOM fall out of your wallet?"

"Jesus Gwen, shut up." Kendra hurried to pay the man for her slice. Gwen became louder.

"Gosh Kendra, I thought just boy virgins carried condoms in their wallets until they expire. How very progressive of you!"

"Uh, actually, it is?" Kendra spat back, scrambling for the condom on the floor while the cashier held her slice, "Women and men should take equal responsibility for birth control, don't you think?"

She'd gotten the condom and two others from the school nurse, figuring nothing could be worse than having the opportunity for sex and not being prepared for it. Kendra had thought herself quite sensible, with no worries or shame. In a busy pizza place, stuck between an impatient cashier and a long line-up of mostly people she knew from school, embarrassment managed to jimmy an opening for regret to find its way in.

"So where are all these boys you're 'sharing responsibility' with, huh Kendra?" Her table of theater friends laughed, "Were they worried the condom wouldn't protect them from your retainer wire?"

"Hey Gwen, it's not her fault if you tired them all out in your never ending quest to break the world dick sucking record." It was Will! Standing four spots behind Kendra, he spoke to the other guys in line, "Yeah, you fellas were all there huh? Phew, you're braver than I am. You know, there's a lot of bacteria in anyone's mouth, but Gwen's? Damn, that's some real germ warfare. Sperm warfare, more like it."

The guys in line, and even a couple of Gwen's more fickle table-mates, began to snicker.

"Fuck you, Will!" It was novel for Kendra to see Gwen lose her cool. Getting out of the way of the next customer, Kendra headed for the door as her former friend continued to shout at her current crush, "You're the one trying to win a dick sucking competition with all those guys on the wrestling team!"

"And what if I was?" Will demurred, putting one hand to his forehead as if feeling faint, "Goodness, all this homophobia in the air. It's unseemly."

More snickers, including Kendra as she passed Will. She wanted to give him a smile or even join in. She couldn't. This big of a public scene was just too much and the sensation of being overwhelmed ballooned when, hearing his voice come closer, she realized Will had left the line to follow her outside.

"Garcon? Garcon?" He shouted to the staff behind the counter, keeping an index finger pointed at Gwen, "This fine young madam has put me off eating at your establishment, what with her homophobia and regressive attitude toward birth control. I shan't return so long as you tolerate such ill-bred harlots!"

"'Garcon' is French, you idiot." Outside, Kendra felt comfortable enough to tease. She had to do something to distract herself from the wild animal thumping against the inside of her sternum.

"What, they don't have pizza in France?" Will replied, the two of them turning left, heading toward a Taco Bell, "Hoo boy, that Gwen, what a wild woman! Next thing you know, she'll be starring in 'Dinosaur Pictures', don't ya think? I wonder which dinosaur she'd be…maybe a Skankasaurs Rex?"

Kendra didn't care for the politics of a lot of what he was saying. She wanted to tell him heterosexual female promiscuity was just as wrong to judge as homosexual male promiscuity, and so what if Gwen ever did end up in pornography? But it was such a breath of fresh air to be stood up for, and she could teach him better, later.

"Are you sure it's okay for me to have food from another restaurant here?" She asked as they got in line.

"'Restaurant'" He snorted, eyes on the menus above the cashiers, "And yeah, screw'em. I mean, what are they gonna do?"

"I guess so." She took a big bite, feeling giddy for what still felt like a transgression, "Thanks for giving Gwen shit, back there.'

"Aw, no problem. I hate bullies. Plus, I dunno, you just seem too cool to be taking crap from the likes of her."

"Really?"

"Yeah, listen - Fiery Doritos Locos Supreme and a large Coke, please - it's okay if I eat lunch with you, right? I feel like I just kind of assumed you would, since you're alone."

"Oh yeah, no, yeah, no, that's cool."

"Cool."

A minute later and they were sitting in a booth Kendra had chosen because booths were supposed to be more romantic, or so stories told her. Having finished most of her pizza by the time they sat down, she watched Will eat and tried to think of something interesting to say that wouldn't make him pull That Face. They'd covered Gwen and there wasn't much more to say about Ms. Rice's sweaters. The Taco Bell was empty of anyone worth making fun of. Kendra was pretty sure his Dad was out of the woods with the cancer, but not sure enough to ask. She'd been reading about sexual surrogates, which would likely weird him out. There'd been some great moments in the latest role-playing game with the guys, though it'd require at least a half hour of preamble before he could even begin to understand why those moments had been so great. This was to say nothing of how he'd probably react to talk of twenty-sided dice and all that came with them. Jesus, why did everything she was enthusiastic about have to put so many people off?

"You're quiet."

"Me? What? That's weird." Kendra gave a short, nervous laugh.

"S'okay. It's nice to be able to just be quiet around people for a minute." He put down the remaining hunk of his taco, "Hey, what are you doing Saturday?"

Sex Offenders Monthly

"So a strange boy wants to take you somewhere in his white van?" Kendra's mother was home and awake during normal hours for a change; usually this would be more appreciated. Sitting in the high-backed, threadbare, brown arm chair they'd had since before Kendra could remember, her mother's short black hair came off as masculine in a way her daughter always thought might be a way of fitting in easier with what was still a male-dominated workplace. This was the only visual reminder of firefighting, as her mom had replaced her usual Grey fire-house t-shirt and sweat pants with a red blouse and hip-hugging dark blue jeans; a date night outfit. She could hear her Dad in the bathroom, washing away the grime and aches of his week's work.

"Mom, he's not strange-"

"I've never heard of him"

"So I gotta report all the guys I know?" Kendra explained it wasn't his fault if what his parents gave him to drive was consistently top-rated in Sex Offenders Monthly, that it came in handy because Will had two brothers and a sister. Besides it wouldn't be the two of them alone, he'd be bringing two friends of his, Owen Forster and Camilla Rosales.

"So you don't know his friends. Are you bringing anybody?"
Kendra just managed to stop herself from saying "No."
"Uh, well, Val was home sick today. Still, I think she'll be up for joining us on Saturday." Her mom didn't look skeptical, yet the feeling was the same, "And Richard's coming too."
Richard was the best choice. A pedantic mall goth geek with a narrow field of interests and a willingness to extend the awkwardness of any situation if it meant he got the last word in an argument, Paul was the trickiest puzzle piece to fit into a different picture. Tim wasn't objectionable in any overt way, yet he was the least curious of the bunch and unlikely to get anything out of a downtown adventure. Plus there was the pool thing.
The last time Kendra had tried to mix friend groups had been when she invited all three of the guys to join her and Val in Gwen's pool, back in Grade Eight. Seeing Val in a bikini gave Tim a boner faster than he could cover it up. Val was so freaked out she leaped from the pool, ran indoors and locked herself in Gwen's bathroom. She insisted on staying in there until the guys left. As close as they were, this was one of the very few things Kendra was forbidden from bringing up. So it was down to Richard, who had decent social skills, an ability to enjoy the world outside of his bubble, and hadn't terrified anybody with his genitals - she hoped.
Kendra's mother mulled over what she'd been told. "Okay. Just try to be back before midnight and don't wake anybody up when you get in, alright?"
"Awesome, yeah, sure." Kendra sunk back into the couch, "Can I have some money to buy dinner and stuff?"

"Didn't your father just give you money for clothes?"

"Yeah, she wants to get more of those Goodwill suits." He said, coming down the stairs. He really had cleaned himself up. Her mother's pupils grew a little wider and a little darker as she went to the front closet, fetching her imitation fur coat. Even if Kendra's father had a pretty cheesy sense of taste in the gifts he chose for his wife, she always appreciated the intention behind them.

"Alright Kay, I'll give you some money on Friday. Don't forget to turn out the lights before you go to bed."

"I won't!"

And then they were gone.

Greg was out with some friends or whatever he was doing.

So.

Thirty minutes later, Kendra lay in bed with her head turned to look at her desk chair, which she'd propped against the door. Tablet glowing in the corner of her vision, she was glad she'd been able to find something on a website which didn't feel too virus-y and even had a man and a woman who were smiling; the amateur stuff tended to be better for that. Sometimes she wished she was brave, or maybe naive, enough to share pictures of herself online. Aside from the horror show of embarrassment bound to ensue if anyone she knew saw them, there was also the thought of getting a lukewarm reception from strangers. It was bad enough when she shared a funny Youtube clip and didn't get any response.

But maybe if she sent something racy to Will, who'd given her his number at the end of lunch, it would have the intended effect? He seemed like he'd be the type to keep it to himself. A few moments of thought, the bluish-white rectangle of light casting her shadow across the room in an even thinner, ganglier, Slenderwoman-ish form, and Kendra decided it wasn't a wise risk to take. Still, it was fun to imagine. A few more moments of thought and she was reaching for the tablet again.

For a moment, Kendra felt a flash of guilt and wondered why she wasn't the way girls were supposed to be with this stuff. Weren't they not supposed to be into pornography? Weren't girls who were horny all the time just a fantasy for boys A.K.A. the ones who were actually supposed to be horny all the time? God, why was she like this? Did she inherit it? Was her mom like this?

"Ew, not cool." Kendra said to her empty bedroom. A brief mental flicker of her parents fondling each other and some half-composed line about "needing that hose of yours to put out my fire" did a pretty good job of killing her interest in a return to the smiling, happy, fucking people who needed to invest in a better tripod and lock their cat in another room while filming. Turning off the tablet, Kendra removed the rest of her clothes and burrowed under the covers. Drifting off, she decided never to feel guilty about her desires ever again. Anything that felt so good or, as it so often did, bittersweet couldn't be something she should feel bad about.

Shitty Phone

Come Saturday morning, Kendra sat on the porch with Spicy Italian wriggling in her lap and a cloth shopping bag between her feet. Snacks, she'd told her parents. Beers, she'd sourced through her brother. Still twenty, he had plenty of friends who were old enough to buy. Problem was, they took a tax and then he took his middleman fee. This was how a six-pack became a four-pack. Kendra hoped Richard was still put off by alcohol and that maybe one of Will's friends wouldn't be thirsty.

Hearing the grumbling of a bus getting back up to speed after a stop, she was pleased to see Val looking hale and hearty as she approached from the t-junction. They hugged, Spicy Italian squirming up from between them to perch on Val's shoulder.

"Dog for weed. Feels like a good deal to me."

"Shhh." Kendra took the three joints Val passed into her hand, pocketing them in a new-to-her brown corduroy blazer. Tiny red polo players atop pale yellow horses chased each other around her tastefully rumpled men's dress shirt, a skinny black tie dividing the eastern and western tribes. Chocolate brown slacks, held up by a belt whose Texas-shaped buckle told the world everything was indeed bigger there, ran down to crumple on the heels of black dress shoes her parents had bought her for an aunt's wedding in the summer.

"It took a lot of convincing to get Nat to part with these." Val had taken some of her sister's more concealing, shapeless clothes and Kendra loved her for it, "Nice belt buckle, I like how it advertises your cavernous cooch."

"No! I just thought it'd be funny to wear something bragging about a big dick, since, you know, I don't have one?" Kendra ran her thumb along the buckle's edge, "It'd have been better if I'd found a buckle saying, like, 'Members Lounge' with an arrow pointing down, like I'm getting crazy dick in there."

"Is that something for a girl to brag about?"

"It should be!" Kendra paused, "If they're into dicks, I guess."

"Well, for now you have all this sausage!" Val gathered Spicy Italian up like a corn cob and buried her face in his belly, to the delight of both parties.

"So okay, I'm thinking maybe at dinner you could help me get a seat beside Will-"

"Mark! Mark! Mark!" Spicy Italian changed his mind about the situation and writhed out of Val's grip, dropping to the ground. The two girls ran after him, enjoying the chase around the lawn before tossing the scrappy pooch indoors.

"Kendra, can I ask a favor?" Val wiped fine brown dog hairs from the lower half of her face.

"Sure?"

"I'm still kinda wiped out from being sick, I've set aside almost my whole Saturday to be your winglady, and we discuss your love life all the time. Can we talk about something else until Will gets here?"

Kendra blushed. Val had a point.

"So anyways," Val tugged at her hoodie's drawstrings, "I've been thinking maybe I'd like to get into making clothes, like, for real."

"Good for you, I bet you'll be great at it!" Kendra tried for puppy dog eyes, "So you'll help me with my costume?"

"Don't worry, I'll-" Seeing her friend's eyes dart to a point over her shoulder, Val abandoned her sentence.

"Hey guys!" Will called out from where he'd parked on the side of the road.

Socks keeping the bottles from clinking, Kendra grabbed her bag and tried not to look too excited as she took long, swift strides toward Will's van. Emboldened by the sight of an otherwise empty vehicle, she gave Val a glance that was greeted by a permissive smile, then sat in the passenger seat while Val pulled open the sliding door and sat in the middle bench, behind Will.

"Hi!" Kendra felt her vision blur a little around the edges, it was hard to look right at Will's face, in a nice way, "I hope you don't mind, but I brought some beers and a few joints for later, maybe?"

"S'alright." Will pulled away, heading toward a corner of the neighborhood Kendra never went to, "Hi Val! Nice to meet you, well, out of school."

"Yeah, you were in my Geography class last year." She replied, "You and Owen always got in trouble for talking too much."

"It was mostly me talking too much to Owen. He's great a guy but too quiet, too shy."

"Nice rap." Seeing a traffic cop cruise by, Kendra moved the bag of beers down between her feet.

"Oh yeah, I guess that rhymed." Will thought for a second, "He's a great guy / too quiet, too shy / a wrestler with brains / so big he never tolerates, uh, hunger pains."

"Oh nice." Val crossed her arms, "Calling your buddy fat."

"Naw, he's just big. Well, okay, he's kinda got a gut. You gotta understand, though, dude has muscles under those snacks."

Forced by speed bumps to crawl along the curve of a crescent, they came to rest at the end of the laneway for a beige-bricked bungalow with a framed Virgin Mary staring back at them from behind the screen door. Her face was replaced with one far less sanguine as Camilla pushed out onto the lawn, synchronizing a scowl with the middle-aged woman peering between the living room curtains to watch her leave. Kendra's eyes were locked on Camilla as well. She hadn't been sure who Will meant when he'd mentioned her; Camilla's outfit cleared things up. Heavy black eye make-up. Dark green lipstick. A half dozen cheap necklaces with symbols from a variety of religions and band logos hanging off them. A butchered second-hand wedding dress, cut to stop just above the knees. Blood-red leggings. Doc Martins. Grey, fingerless gloves made from lace. She was one of Azealia's friends.

Everyone felt it in their ears when Camilla, scooting in beside Val, slammed the sliding door shut.

"Hey Will." She said, "I love my momma so much, you know? She's just fan-tast-ic."

"So you've told me." Will grinned, pulling away to go pick up Richard. Kendra saw Camilla's mother stock still in the window of their home, eyes tracking the van like a painting in a corny horror film. As unsettling as this was, she preferred to focus on something specific so it might seem more natural that she hadn't greeted Camilla when she'd taken a seat beside Val. Whatever the truth of the situation, it already felt like there was a patch of heat on the back of her neck from Camilla shooting lasers out of her eyes.

"Anyways…" Will continued, "This is Kendra, up here with me, and beside you there is her best friend, Val."

Kendra raised one arm to give a weak, back-of-the hand, wave hello. Both people in the front of a vehicle had to pay attention to the road at all times or they might crash, right? Either of them looking back at the passengers would be too risky, right?

"Oh yeah, Kendra, I've seen you with Val." Camilla turned to her left, "Hey Val."

"Hey."

Camilla quickly began laughing with Will about inside jokes and stories Kendra couldn't decode. Stealing the odd glance at Val through the rear-view mirror, the two friends mostly sat in silence until they saw the large, plastic toys and play structures dominating Richard's front lawn. These had been a fixture ever since his parents had given him a surprise little sister twelve whole years after they'd brought him into the world. Playing board games with Richard and Paul in the living room, Kendra had overheard his father's reaction even though he'd been behind closed doors, on the other end of the house. Apparently he'd had a vasectomy after Richard was born and was vexed to be reminded there was still a small possibility of getting someone pregnant even after the procedure. Thinking of his thickly thatched chest hair, strong chin and powerful thighs, Kendra liked to imagine Richard's dad had gotten his wife pregnant through sheer force of handsomeness.

Poor Richard, with his weak, hairless chin and skinny legs, didn't seem to have inherited any of that, which may have been why he reacted poorly to Kendra trying to tease him with 'hot dad' comments a few years later. She'd just been trying to play a similar game to what Paul and Richard often started whenever Tim's Olympian sister passed by, her seemingly having taken a vow to wear top's so tight they had to be rolled on like a condom. Maybe it was thoughts of Tim's sister which had Richard, sitting on his two-story home's doorstep, daydreaming so hard he hadn't noticed Will's van pulling up.

"Hey Richard!" Kendra called out to him, "Come on down!'

"Oh, uh, hey!" he called back, "Sorry, guess I failed my hearing check again." Kendra laughed. In last week's RPG session, Richard's computer hacker hadn't heard a guard dog sneak up behind him. Its teeth sinking into his butt had set off a fiasco that derailed the game for hours in a Keystone Kops kind of way; everyone at the table holding their stomachs with laughter. She loved having this kind of shorthand with someone, a single reference bringing her back to both an exciting, detailed world of fantasy as well as the comfortable good times of sitting around a table with old friends.

She was also glad nobody else in the van heard what Richard said.

It hadn't been hard to convince Val to come along; Richard

took more work. He'd never admit it to anyone other than Kendra, but Will made Richard feel less than confidant. Seeing things from his point of view, Kendra could understand how a self-assured guy on the wrestling team could be intimidating, especially when he had a cute girlfriend who dressed like something out of any number of Anime or Manga Richard was into.

Ex-girlfriend. Far away ex-girlfriend. Basically a dead person. Basically.

Richard slid the door open, trying to hide his unease around Camilla - an unfamiliar girl. He greeted everyone before settling into the back bench seat, right behind Val. It wasn't far from Richard's house to a newer, nicer stretch of the local suburbs where three story houses and backyard pools started to appear. The home where they stopped to pick up Owen even had a brand new luxury sedan in the laneway.

The van settled a little lower as he got in to sit in the back with Richard. Slumped shoulders. Not quite looking ahead. Hands hanging limply at his sides. Kendra, recognizing how she'd carried herself up until not too long ago, felt sympathy for this pudgy, 6'4 giant in his bed sheet of a plain brown t-shirt and baggy cargo pants. Like Camilla when she'd first appeared, he didn't look too happy, however his sour mood seemed here to stay.

"Hey."

"Hey man!" Will replied, "You alright? You weren't answering any of my texts yesterday."

"Yeah." Owen sighed, "It's all good. Just…forgot to charge my shitty phone, you know?"

"Okay, cool cool. Shitty Phone is such a bad brand." Will went on to introduce everybody. Richard made a point of shaking Owen's hand, regret flitting across his face when Camilla, grinning, insisted on shaking his hand as well as Val's. Soon they were on the highway, suburbs falling away behind them like a boring dream about room-temperature microwave lasagna.

Window rolled down, sitting high above most of the surrounding traffic, Kendra felt her senses sharpen and her skin tingle when she realized this would be her first trip downtown without her parents. Until now they hadn't been okay with letting her go on her own, while neither she nor her brother were excited by the idea of his being put in charge of her for several hours. It wasn't New York, Tokyo, or London. Relative to her life experiences, with little more than the mandatory Disneyland adventure and a few trips to see friends of the family in Maine, it was close enough to crank up the contrast in her fantasies about those far away cities. As they came to the off-ramp, the buildings grew taller and so did Kendra as she craned her neck.

"This is exciting." She said to nobody in particular.

"Do you not get downtown often?" Will asked.

"No." She'd thought about lying to look cooler, then decided she didn't want to be dishonest with him, "Almost never, really."

"Oh! Well I was going to park at the Sharrett Center and figured we could just go wherever. Is that cool, or did you have something in mind?"

Much as with Will, Kendra was excited enough by downtown in a general sense to not want anything specific than to be in its presence.

"Uh, no. I'm good for making things up as we go along." Kendra kept her eyes on Will, "How about you guys?"

Richard shrugged, Owen wanted to go to the Army Surplus store for a new backpack, and Val wanted to get dinner anywhere that wasn't a chain.

"Yeah, what Val said." Camilla added.

They pulled into the five story parking lot of the Sharrett Center, Kendra enjoying the feeling as they spiraled up and up and up. Will found a spot in the far corner of the uppermost floor of the lot, with a view that made Kendra drum her fingers on her knee in anticipation. Looking at the skyscrapers and condo buildings looming over the old market area where they'd spend most of their time, Kendra wanted to grow powerful claws in her hands and feet so she could climb up to the corners of the grandest of these structures, cut through a window and crawl inside to make a nest for herself. She wanted to find the perfect bar to live above, deep in the marketplace, where she could keep an eye on all the latest trends in clothing, food, and culture. She wanted both at the same time, plus a job which didn't require her to get up before noon, so she could spend every evening living an exciting nightlife full of imagery pieced together from articles online, indie films, social media, stories she'd heard, and her imagination.

She could not see her house from here.

Will smiled. "Hey, you want to have those beers now?"

"What?" Richard said.

"I guess if we're quick about it…" Kendra said, turning to look back at the others, "But I only have four."

"I'm alright, just one beer won't do much for me." Owen told them. Richard pulled a face, letting Kendra know his feelings about drinking hadn't changed. She slid the bottles from their sock wrappings in the bag and handed one each out to Will, Val, and Camilla. Will went to remove the cap on his, couldn't. Shit! She hadn't even checked to see if they were screw-offs or not.

Will shrugged and pulled a Swiss Army Knife, which of course he had, from a jacket pocket. Soon they were all enjoying their drinks, Val grinning at Kendra and Kendra just beaming. With the view and the company, cheap beers in a multi-level parking lot of a city with a population of barely a million felt like fine whiskey in the New York Grill at the top floor of Park Hyatt Tokyo.

"Oh crap." Will looked out his side window at something Kendra couldn't see, "A parking lot employee's coming toward us. Quick, finish your drinks!"

Richard's face went red, while Owen just grinned as he watched the others chug their beers. Val got a little on her sweater. Bottle tipped high, Camilla gave Will stink-eye the entire time.

"Come on guys, hurry up!"

Kendra took a deep breath through her nose as she guzzled away, hoping the sound of it wasn't too gross. Just as she finished, the last to do so, Will glanced outside again.

"Oh no wait, sorry, there's nobody at all and there never was. Oops!"

"Screw you Will! God, I knew you were doing that again."

Camilla said, gesturing to the sides of the van interior, "I just couldn't see because this old Uhaul bullshit doesn't have any side windows back here."

Will smile-shrugged to his friend. Val belched. Camilla, laughing, handed her empty bottle up front. Empties collected in the cloth shopping bag, they all piled out, Kendra feeling a not-unpleasant weight in her temples. As they crossed the short distance to the elevator, she pulled Val aside and whispered in her ear.

"Was Camilla, like, staring daggers at me for sitting beside Will? 'Cause she's friends with Azealia, you know?"

Val shook her head, gave another small burp. "Barely looked at you, I wouldn't worry."

"So, uh, where are we going first?" Richard asked.

Are You a Believer?

They wandered along Price Street, a major avenue running parallel with the market and the mall. Kendra was reminded how, for better or worse, the area where she lived was so much emptier than here. Far fewer pedestrians. No buskers. No homeless people, that could be seen. A dearth of people in their twenties, except service industry employees. She knew what was found on the streets of downtown wasn't all good, that a great deal of it was awful, but it was all good by her.

Will and Camilla directed them to a modest storefront which did nothing to prepare Val, Kendra and Richard for the scope and grandeur of the inside. Rock Highway had a treasure hoard of band posters, belts, framed and signed photographs of rock stars from before their parents were born, electric guitars more artifact than instrument, and even a few Halloween masks all hanging from floor to two story high ceiling. Glass cabinets and cases made up most of the floorspace, displaying costume jewelery, primary colored hair dyes, still more belts, glass pipes, novelty lighters with lines from old movies or rubber-limbed 1920's cartoon characters on them, bracelets, necklaces like Camilla wore, fingerless leather gloves, and even a few underground comics Kendra felt herself drawn to.

Richard checked out the posters, Camilla looked at more necklaces to add to her collection, Owen seemed to spend an eternity contemplating a jar of aquamarine hair dye he didn't end up buying, Val picked up a lighter with Betty Boop on the side for her sister, and Kendra was relieved to be allowed to buy two reprints of old "Cherry" comics. The art and title font was almost identical to the old Dan Dicarlo style which had dominated Archie Comics for half a century, the look most people associated with them even after the company had started being more adventurous, breaking from their house style to try other North American and Manga-inspired takes on their timeless characters.

"Oh my God, porno Archies?" Will said, seeing Kendra flicking through one of her finds. It was true, Cherry seemed to come from an alternate universe version of Riverdale where everyone - her in particular - was oversexed and happy to do something about it.

"Yeah, crazy huh?" Kendra replied, thrilled to hear from his tone he was as amused and interested in the find as she was. Kevin or Scott, or Gwen for that matter, would have just given her That Look, as if they'd been stunned into silence by how violently the conversation died at the hands of Kendra's eccentric interests. "Look at her, she's eating out the principal's wife and two pages later she's having a threesome with them both."

"This." Will put his index finger on the panel, "This is just so true to life, you know?"

Kendra laughed. "Right? Every time I go to the office I have to have a threesome with the principal and his wife, who I guess is there because she has nothing better to do, when I'm all 'I just came here to…sigh, oh, okay I guess. Geez.' It's such a hassle."

Will chuckled, "How very accommodating of you."

"Well, you know me." Kendra closed the comic, "I live to please."

Will didn't buy anything, thwarting Kendra's plans to compliment him on whatever it could have been. The backs of their hands nearly touched as they squeezed out onto the sidewalk, so she made a note to keep an eye out for any further narrow passages they might encounter. From there they crossed through a McDonald's. Kendra was delighted by their playing Beethoven so loud it could be heard on the sidewalk.

"They do it to keep people from hanging around the doors." Will told her, noticing the joyous curiosity on her face, "Funny thing is, it works."

On the other side of the McDonald's they came into the market proper. A relic from when the city had started as a small trading post, supplying travelers on the way to try their luck in the California gold rush or heading south-west to cattle country, the market had been preserved for historical reasons and so the wealthier downtown residents could enjoy the illusion of small town shopping. Set up semi-permanently along widened sidewalks, there were stalls selling all kinds of fruits and vegetables, as well as food trucks who'd figured out how to charge more for a large, well made saltwater pretzel or single portion of duck fat fries than Kendra was used to spending on an entire meal from the school cafeteria.

Plump saltwater pretzels in hand, Kendra, Val and Richard

entered a vinyl toy boutique, Vinyl Poseur, and were surprised to see Camilla follow them inside. Will and Owen were next door, amusing themselves by providing ridiculous dialog for the assortment of unusual creatures in the tanks of an exotic seafood shop.

Back in Vinyl Poseur, white floors, walls, shelves and ceiling made it a little easier to sort through the carnival of two to twelve inch figures. Robots. Animals. Monsters. Chibi versions of all the major Anime characters. A cartoon band her Dad sometimes wore t-shirts of. An entire, fourteen figure line of anthropomorphic turds. They had it all!

"Nice outfit!" the clerk complimented Camilla, who just looked at him and nodded. She knew.

A Batman figure perched on the highest shelf, standing alongside a sign reminding customers shoplifting would get them sent straight to Blackgate Prison. Looking at the prices, Kendra figured she almost would have to shoplift if she wanted to get a figure and still have a comfortable amount of money left for dinner. Man, she needed to work out a way to make some more money on the side.

"Things seemed to be going well back in Rock Highway." Val whispered, sidling up beside Kendra while Richard and Camilla checked out different corners of the store.

"Yeah." Kendra whispered back, fondling a zombie bear-cub figure with a head as big as its torso, "I can make him laugh. But what about the other…stuff?"

"Well, do you get a feeling when he's close?"

"Definitely. I just can't tell if he does?"

Then they both had to pretend something else was being discussed, as Camilla came over to the same set of shelves they were standing by.

"Hey, do either of you buy these ones?" she asked Kendra and Val, pointing to a long rectangle made up of blueprint patterned boxes bearing large white question marks overlayed on generic Chibi silhouettes in black. As the packaging suggested, their contents were randomly determined, making it more challenging to collect the entire set of creatures. Kendra had four of them on a bookshelf in her bedroom.

"Yeah, I've got Excreto Supreme, Robo-Router and, uh, two of the little guy with six legs." She answered.

"Spider-zoid, yeah. I'm gonna buy some of these and, if I get one I already have, that you need, can I trade you for a Spider-zoid? I just need him and a Tony Enigmatic to finish the set."

"Holy crap! Almost the whole set?"

"I don't know how you guys can buy those without knowing what you're getting." Val told them.

"It's part of the fun, Val." Kendra grabbed a couple of question-marked cubes for herself.

"Yeah, Valium." Camilla took six and then they all headed to the cash.

"Valium?" Valerie asked.

"You've been kinda sleepy and slow all day today." Camilla explained, "I couldn't help noticing."

Richard was just in the middle of being served as they all came up behind him. He'd selected a ten inch anime character wielding twin shotguns and wearing a Gothic Lolita style outfit.

"Hey, you're buying a little me!" Camilla said, copying the pose while making pistols with her hands to substitute for shotguns. She gave a big smile. Richard shrank into his shirt.

Purchases made, they went outside to rejoin Will and Owen before heading to the army surplus store. Children's sized gas masks, canteens, and rucksacks sat in large, square wire bins arranged around the front doors like improvised sandbag defenses.

Inside, narrow corridors stroked passing customs with the arms of countless jackets; a forest of browns, greens and navy blues broken up by the rare splash of orange on the end of a toy gun or gunmetal grey along the edge of a knife in a locked display case. Everything hanging from the two-tier, floor-to-ceiling clothing racks looked - and often smelled - like they'd been made out of old tents unpacked from an extended period in a storage locker. Bucket helmets and adult sized gas masks filled a few more wire bins. Above these were smaller plastic bins on a high shelf, filled with badges for organizations and armies requiring years of intensive training to join. All it took to get a badge was a few dollars.

Val decided this wasn't her thing and went across the street to a candy store, Sweet Fever's Classy Confectionery. Kendra figured Camilla must have felt the same way, since she pulled a bit of a face at a collection of waterproof ponchos before turning around and leaving as well. Owen's ponderous bulk blocked off access to Will, the pair of them looking at olive-green backpacks in a far corner, so Kendra went to look at badges with Richard.

He was eying a fabricated U.S. Marine Corps Rifle Expert qualification badge, she assumed because he always played as a sniper in Hat Wars Three and all the other online shooters they played in. Noticing Kendra, Richard turned to pick up a scratched, dark grey bucket helmet, “Hey, how many points of ballistic protection do you think this one would give you?”

“Like, two. One point of impact as well, I think. ” Kendra thought for a second, “Only on hit locations three and four, there’s no face or neck coverage.”

“What if I put it here?” Richard placed the helmet over his left thigh and Kendra laughed. The rules of the role-playing game system they’d been using for the past year involved rolling two dice and consulting a table to see where a player hit a person on their body when they attacked them. Almost half the time they’d roll somewhere from seven to eleven, meaning a person would be hit in the left thigh. Soon their games featured complex theories about the left thigh being the true home of the soul, left thigh medical specialists and, in Paul’s fantasy campaign, Kendra founded an order of paladins who had trouble walking because of how heavily armored their left thighs were; they had a tendency to move in broad circles and were suspicious of anyone with a thigh gap.

“What’s so funny about wearing a helmet on your leg?” Valerie asked.

“Oh, nothing, really.” Kendra felt bad for not wanting to explain this to her friend, felt even worse when she realized she was guilty of thinking in terms of something like Gwen’s ‘levels’ with the way she kept so many partitions between the world of her gaming pals and other friends who registered as ‘cooler’ in one way or another, “You’re back quickly.”

"Yeah." Val looked absentmindedly at a pistol lighter, "I dunno. Didn't really want candy that badly."

Camilla's hand landed on Valerie's shoulder. "Hey guys, I'm hungry, you wanna find somewhere to eat?"

If there was one thing the market had, it was places to eat and drink. 1950's diners. Sushi. Italian, authentic and franchise. Tapas. Kendra tried to make her being glued to Will's side seem a natural result of the current of the crowd. Two blocks over from where they'd been shopping, Will and Owen spotted a dive bar they thought they'd be able to sneak into. Its exterior was painted dark grey by the owners, with sooty black highlights provided by years of accumulated air pollution. Standing by the door was a very tall man who wasn't having much luck getting spare change from customers when he held the door for them.

"Are you guys kidding?" Camilla said, "Owen might be the size of a truck, but we're not convincing anybody we're of age. Besides, Richard's obviously nervous about that guy holding the door for people."

He obviously was, though Kendra didn't think Camilla had to say it out loud. Heck, she was a little nervous as well. Not getting any money didn't seem to be improving the tall man's mood.

"Oh my God, guys! Turn around!" Val drew their attention to a place not far down from the dive bar. Sixties surf music was pouring out of a half-open window. A chalkboard sign standing by the door promised a broad variety of Asian, American, and Mexican foods as well as over thirty kinds of vodka. Painted across its storefront window was a mural of ten people and one empty chair sitting around a blue table with a black opening in the middle. The floor around the table was painted white, surrounded by yellow, in a shape Kendra realized would look like an eye if she had a top-down view instead of the low, three quarter angle the artist had chosen. The diners in the mural were from all around the world, with clothing a polyglot of cultures, colors and time periods. Standing much closer to the fourth wall, there was a man dressed in what Kendra took to be a style of Catholic priest's robes, eyes hidden by a tall, rounded hat with a wide brim. Gesturing from under his robes, the mustachioed priest drew attention to the one empty chair at the table and, in a font she now wanted to know the name of, invited Kendra and the others to come in and dine at The Holy Mountain.

"That's insane." Kendra said to nobody in particular, "We have to eat there."

Val nodded her head, agreeing with both statements. The two went in, Camilla following Val, and the guys trailing after.

"*Whoa,*" Kendra thought, *"It's like a clubhouse for adults."*

Dark, recycled wood paneling made uniform with a rosewood lacquer provided the base layer for walls covered in framed posters of campy exploitation films from the sixties and seventies. As they stepped onto cracked linoleum, surf music switched to French pop from the same era. A bar ran along the left side, and booths along the right. Through a doorway at the back was a large, semi-private room with a painted yellow floor and iconic eyeball table just like they'd seen in the mural. Kendra knew where she wanted everyone to sit.

"We normally reserve that room for large groups." The waitress, a doe eyed woman whose shaved head and purple suit were modeled on one of the dinner guests in the mural, told them, "But it's pretty quiet, so you lovelies can have it."

As they were led to the table, Kendra couldn't help herself. "I like your suit! It's so…crisp."

"Thanks." The waitress smiled at her, tapping the shoulder of Kendra's blazer, "I like yours even better."

As they took their seats, Valerie noticed the black iris of the table was a hole covered in plexi-glass.

"What's this, like, exactly?" she asked.

"It's better to show you." The waitress replied, "And I know just which one to choose."

"Which what to choose?" Richard asked of the others, after she had left the room to fiddle with something under the bar. Soon a blue-ish white light shot from the iris and they all looked up at a ceiling painted with white projection screen paint. A moment later and they saw a young Jane Fonda slowly spinning, silently doing a zero gravity disrobe. The set looked like their school drama club props people had assembled it from the leftover stock of a fake fur warehouse.

"Barbarella. It's a classic." The waitress told them as she returned, "Now what can I get you to drink?"

A small meter inside Kendra's brain, with 'Greg Sitting on my Head and Farting' at the very bottom, shot straight up to 'Best Anything Ever' and stayed there for the entire meal. Everything about the restaurant was novel and exciting. She was able to sit beside Will. Everyone got along with each other and had plenty to say, even Owen and Richard. Camilla continued to reveal herself to not only not be hostile toward Kendra, she was outright friendly and possibly willing to wade into deeper, nerdier territory than even her taste for collectible toys had suggested. The food had a home cooked feel, enhanced by the thrift store plates and cutlery. Will lent her twenty dollars to cover her Pad Thai when Kendra realized she'd overspent at Vinyl Poseur. His left hand glanced off her right no less than four times. She made him laugh more than she could keep track of. Kendra hugged herself and smiled when they were heading back out.

Dusk was making its daily debut as they came outside and stood in a circle, trying to figure out what they wanted to do next.

"Hey, are you a member of the Church?"

It was the tall guy who'd been holding the door at the dive bar. He looked ancient to Kendra, a mixture of age and living rough, with his knotty white goatee growing down to just above a very pronounced Adams apple. Hair unseen, yet surely ample, filled a bulbous black toque. His limbs were long, with hard, dangerous looking joints, and a wiry strength to them which was apparent even beneath loose, black winter clothing. Now he was standing very close to Will, having tapped on his shoulder.

"Haha, what?" Will said.

"Are you a believer of Scientology?"

"Oh!" Will turned to face him, "No, naw man those people are idiots. I-"

"You've been following me for them." The man stuck a finger in Will's chest like he was testing the temperature of a freshly baked pie, "And I want you to stop."

"Uh," Will rubbed his chest where he'd been poked, "okay. You have my word, I'll stop."

The man gave another poke, retreating a foot right after he did so. Knees bent, his deep-set eyes never leaving Will's. Kendra looked to Camilla, who held no solutions to their situation.

"I want you to stop!" the man screamed, drawing himself up to full height, "I want you to leave!"

"Okay, we're leaving." Will said, getting a gob of spit on his coat in reply. Exhaling loudly through this nose, Will stayed facing the man as he gestured to the others and began walking down the street.

The man followed, hovering about a foot away from Will the whole time. Knees bent again as if ready to spring, he took another cautious poke, "I want you to leave!"

Unsure, Will put out an open hand to keep some space between them. Kendra glanced around, frustrated none of the few pedestrians nearby were doing anything except getting on with their day or stopping to take pictures with their phones. Still, she didn't think she'd want to get involved if she were them. What ate up most of her attention, after the man himself, was noticing Richard and Valerie had fled. They didn't seem to have gone back into The Holy Mountain or any of the other nearby stores and restaurants, they'd just vanished. The man's voice was getting louder, the cadence of his speech rising and falling with the fluctuations of whatever was raging inside him.

"Why don't you leave? You should be leaving! The things you people did to me, you oughta-"

KUNCH

Owen's fist burst open the man's nose, sending him staggering several steps to land on his back in the middle of the street. Kendra looked from the man to Owen, could tell he already felt bad about it. She wondered if all day something hadn't been rising and falling within him as well, and he'd just kept a tighter lid on it until now.

"Dude, we gotta go." Will grabbed his friend's arm.

"Yeah." Owen replied, taking a puff from an asthma inhaler before turning to run with the rest of them.

All the nooks and crannies of the market which had been ripe with exciting possibilities now became places for the man, or someone like him, to be lurking. Kendra could tell he wasn't a monster, yet this did little to stamp down her fear of what he might do if he ever got up - none of them having looked back to see if he had - or her anxiety over the police getting involved. The empty beer bottles waiting for them back in the van took on a new significance. When they got back, not slowing down to walking speed until they'd entered the parking lot, Kendra pulled out the brown paper bag with its sock-wrapped empties and placed it on the ground. Losing a few old socks was the least of her worries.

Driving up onto the highway, they all stared at anything but each other.

"Jesus, Val!" Kendra broke the silence, "Also, Richard."

Pulling out her phone, she saw her best friend had already

texted her. "Richard got scared and ran. Too real. Didn't feel right leaving him, so I followed. We're on the 97, don't worry. You okay?"

"Yeah, we're good. Owen punched the guy, it was nuts! Back in the van now."

Kendra didn't have to wait long for a reply.

"Whoah! Glad you're okay. I'm going home. You?"

"Dunno".

"Okay. Good luck with Will!"

Kendra watched the streetlights come on as they slowed down to fit with the flow of Saturday rush hour.

"God, does anybody have any weed?" Camilla asked.

"Oh, I have some!" Kendra replied, not sure if it was cool to be so excited. She was just pleased to have an excuse to keep the day from ending on such a jarring note.

"You okay, Owen?" Will asked. It took his friend a while to answer.

"Yeah."

"Let's go to the woods by the school and smoke up. I need it."

"Woo!" Camilla raised her arms to touch the roof of the van, looked at Owen, "Woo?"

"Woo." Owen raised his hands to shoulder height.

Not seeing a smile, Camilla gave him a hug. "I need an exclamation mark on that 'Woo', buddy."

Owen let out a one note laugh, providing a smile Camilla accepted in lieu of more woo.

A Pervert You Want to Kiss

Twenty minutes later and Kendra, as Will led them through the woods by the school, was trying to act like she had no idea where they were going. When they arrived, he showed her the cooler.

"Wow, what an awesome idea." She told him.

"Yeah. It keeps the beer nicer than if I left it in my van and is a much better hiding spot. Sometimes I'll have a beer at lunch, but mostly it's for bush parties."

"Those must be pretty fun."

"Oh yeah." Will lifted the lid on the cooler to reveal a sea of empties, "We tore through these pretty fast last Sunday."

"Yeah, we ran out in what? An hour?" Camilla took a seat, still keeping a maternal eye on Owen. Kendra watched him rub his bruised knuckles.

They sat in a circle around the cooler like it was a campfire, sharing first one, then another of the joints Kendra had. Twice in the conversation, Owen spoke over Kendra. Realized she'd suffered a misfire before the sentence was even finished, seasoning what she'd said with much more stank than intended, Kendra blurted out "Stop interrupting me!"

She'd only been trying to keep to her new resolution.

"Fuck, Kendra, no need to get shitty with me. What the hell?" Owen said, showing a little bit of whatever flared up in the middle of the street at the marketplace.

"Whoa, dude, relax." Will told him, "Kendra's just feeling on edge after crazy guy there. So it's a good thing we have the perfect solution right here at our fingertips, don't you think?"

"Well, maybe." Kendra said, thinking "*But my complaint was valid?*"

Once again he was defending her and, in Will's dismissing her complaint by pointing to her emotions, there was something objectionable with how he did so. Once again, she still appreciated someone speaking up for her. She'd read people saying online that they enjoyed problematic shows. Was there such a thing as enjoying problematic boys? Where did she draw the line?

Owen paused, then nodded. "Sorry for interrupting you, Kendra."

"Oh hey, no problem." Kendra grabbed the lit joint and took a deep pull, holding it in as long as she could before breathing it out back through her nose. She tried to sound knowledgeable by asking if they were smoking sativa or indica, not impressing anyone with these words she knew from the Internet. Will, letting her know she was doing well for her first time, showed her how to better absorb the THC, and patted her on the back when the inevitable coughing fit happened. Soon, the clouding of her thoughts obscured the unpleasantness of earlier.

"Well." Camilla stood up, "I'm pretty tired. Owen, it's kinda dark and I still feel rattled. Can you walk with me to the bus stop?"

Owen said he would. After Camilla shot down Will's suggesting he drive them, she exchanged numbers with Kendra, saying they should hang out some time. Surprised, but not as much as she'd have been at the start of the day, Kendra waved goodbye as Will's friends left.

"So." Will said after half a minute of silence, "You wanna light up another one?"

"Maybe later. I'm pretty good right now." Kendra replied, hearing the foggy, distant murmurs of the voice which had kept her from talking to Will so many times in the past. She could almost ignore it.

Almost.

"Random encounter, bitches." Paul's voice came from her phone; on a dare she'd set it to be her general text alert. Kendra saw a message from Camilla.

"Hey mamacita, I'm getting Owen to come on the bus with me so you can be alone with Will. Go for it."

Putting away her phone, Kendra felt like all her senses had become heightened. Open. Receptive.

She needed a line. A move. Something to distract. She stood up and Will, looking curious, did the same.

"Hey." Kendra said, "I just had a really good idea!"

Grabbing his coat's collar, Kendra wrote off a middle school mishap at the one dance she ever attended, deciding this would count as her fist kiss. A half-second thought of how it might lead to another big first, and she was surprised by a jolt of fear. Instinctively she rebelled against the feeling, pushing away from it like a swimmer propelling up off the bottom of a pool toward the shimmering light at the surface. Her lips spread against his, which stayed very still, closed, and dry.

"Thank you." Will said, as if she'd handed him a glass of warm tap water. Trying for a better result, she kissed him again, harder, and lifted a leg to wrap around him the way she'd seen Azealia do. Losing her balance, the force of her kiss sent the pair of them falling forward onto the ground, Will's shoulders taking the brunt of the impact. Pulling her face back, Kendra laughed and smiled, expecting him to do the same.

He did not laugh.

He did not smile.

"You know, I have a girlfriend."

"Had, Will." Kendra said, "You had a girlfriend."

Azealia wasn't just in another town. Kendra had tried to look up Greenville, discovering it was tied for the second most common place name in America. In her mind, Azealia was diffused into a gas, one thirtieth of her volume collecting in thirty cities and towns across twenty-seven states. All those tiny clouds felt far less real and threatening than one whole girl in one specific place. Although, if she were meat and bone and in a single place then at least she could get hit by a car or stabbed by a knife-wielding maniac. Not that Kendra wanted that or anything.

"We're long-distance now." He said, "We talk all the time online. We even started, you know…doing things in front of each other."

This was not what was supposed to happen when a guy and a girl fell to the ground on top of each other. Laughter. Smiles.

Maybe a few shy words, and then smooches. Kinky confessions involving other people, not so much. She knew stories lied to her all the time; the betrayal still stung. Why would he tell her that? Was he too proud to keep it to himself?

"Well, she's an image on a screen now, she's, like, basically just pornography. I'm right here."

"Look, it's not as if I don't think you're cute. Still, again, I'm with someone." His gaze went hard, "I won't cheat on her."

She kissed him again, and again and again. Sure it was wrong, but who knew how long it would be before her lips would touch anybody else? Not knowing meant *knowing* it would be *forever*, that she'd have no *control* over when, and any issue of morality was obscured by the blue shades of those thoughts swirling around with warm streaks of autumnal-

"Okay! Enough." Will gently rolled her off him and sat up, "God, I knew you were a freak when I saw you watching me and Azealia make out."

"And you didn't say anything?!" Kendra stared between branches at the stars before sitting upright and sputtering, "What are you…you liked being watched?"

He didn't say anything.

"Pervert!"

"A pervert you want to kiss!" Will stood again, took a few paces and turned to face her like a Russian Commissar catching a soldier fleeing the front lines. Kendra wanted to stand up, square her shoulders and point right back at him, her index finger the firing sight for a devastating retort whose sheer force of righteousness would unhinge the limbs from his body.

"Go away." Was what she managed, pulling her knees close, burying her face as far she could into her own lap.

"Oh, hey." He came over and put a hand on her shoulder, "I'm sorry, I didn't mean-"

"Leave me alone!" She smacked his hand away, the impact like a cap gun going off, fresh pain causing her voice to wobble, "Please."

"Geez. Okay, I get it."

"Go," Her voice became a raspy growl as she tried to push out all the hurt inside, "awayyyy-uh."

So he did. Kendra didn't see the look on his face. She never wanted to see him again. She'd see him first thing on Monday morning. She owed him twenty bucks.

Still.

This was the first time a boy had told her he found her attractive. Kendra filed this away, a lit candle in the dark.

Still.

She wasn't big on consolation prizes. This information would make her feel better later. Right now it was dwarfed by rejection and hopelessness.

Kendra went over and looked in the cooler. There, among almost two dozen empties, a single bottle had escaped consumption. It was not quite cold, not quite body temperature; it was just right. Pulling the last of Nat's joints from her jacket pocket, Kendra lay back among the leaves and worked her way through the contents of green glass and white paper. Pulled from another jacket pocket, her phone and ear buds brought some calming music to accompany her consumables. Kendra was done with her head and her heart for the moment, so she tried to live in just her lungs, throat, and ears. The battery on her phone ran out about the same time as the liquid and the smoke. The dullness in her head showed mercy by staying.

She got up on stiff joints and threw her empty bottle at the trees right behind where Will and Azealia had been exploring each other. The sound of the smash echoing through the woods, causing all the squirrels to look up from what they were doing.

She refused to feel bad about any of this.

MediaConsumptionCon

The next time Kendra came downtown it was in the family sedan with her Dad at the wheel. Paul, Richard and Tim sat in the backseat. Paul had built on his usual heavy metal clothing with extra spikes and buckles, applied white face paint with a corona of black lines tracing out from each of his eyes, and built a styrofoam and cardboard necromancer's staff modeled after one used by his favorite Wizard Bastards character. The staff lay across the laps of Richard and Tim, both dressed in their usual uniforms of jeans and a t-shirt. Richard's was plain white. Tim's was pale grey with an illustration of an ambulatory fortress belching steam while stalking across alpine wilderness.

Kendra, wrapped up in a heavy winter coat, wore her old red polo shirt and palest blue jeans. In her lap sat a backpack, stuffed with cost-saving snacks, a thermos, toiletries, and the Erica Elastic costume her and Val - mostly Val - had been working on together for the past month. Her wallet was full of cash saved at another of what she'd begun calling 'burner jobs'. This time she'd worked three and a half weeks of part-time, selling Mom jeans at an outlet store embedded among the stretch of strip malls near her neighborhood. Valerie once came by to say hello during a period with no customers in the store. Her boss had said it was okay if she chatted for a while, then took thirty minutes off her pay for the day without telling her he would. In what might have been a related incident, Kendra hadn't seen the need to make up a fanciful lie or even tell him anything at all when it came time to quit without giving two weeks notice.

Mom jeans were the furthest thing from her mind as her father hunted for a spot in the underground parking lot of their town's prize gem, the Martha Steiger Convention Center, named after some self-made property oligarch who'd been born nearby.

"Does everybody have their printed tickets?" Kendra's Dad asked, scoring a corner spot near the entrance.

"Yes Dad. You know they can just scan the email right off our phone's screens."

"Sure, then one of you forgets to charge your phone or their scanner doesn't work."

Ten minutes later they walked around to the convention center's south entrance and joined with a crowd by the doors, almost half of which were in costumes from a variety of game, show, and film franchises, or even their imaginations.

"Ahhhh, my God, look at her!" Kendra said, staring at a woman who'd blended Iron Man with Margaret Thatcher to make an Iron Lady costume, "This is gonna be so awesome."

Kendra was soon in a modest hotel room above the convention, something her parents had been willing to pay for since it meant they didn't have to drive downtown twice as much in order for Kendra to attend both days. She'd be sharing it with a girl two years younger than her, named Celine, who she'd been Internet friends with for a few months. They'd met in the comment threads of a fan-fiction blog they were both too shy to contribute to, and were looking forward to seeing each other in person for the first time. Celine didn't seem to have been by their room yet, so her dad needed some reassuring Kendra would be careful before she was able to hurry him out the door. Then it was time to unpack her costume.

Laying each piece on the cream colored bed spread, Kendra gave them a final once over. Video game characters rarely had any seams on their clothing and, as in the case of Erica Elastic, the women often looked like it was just painted on, with no bunching in the armpits or elsewhere. There was still some faint super glue residue around the bottom of the power crystal, otherwise she was pretty happy with what Val had made for her. Kendra licked her thumb and rubbed off as much as she could. Really, the costume wasn't missing anything except an owner confident enough to wear it in public.

"Like, half of everyone is here in a costume." She said to her outfit, as if it was the one having self-esteem issues, "And it's not like most of them have perfect bodies or costumes. Before coming up here you saw a short, balding Superman and a Wolverine who's claws were all floppy."

Bringing her hands together in one loud clap, a starting pistol for the race to stay ahead of her insecurities, Kendra changed quickly. To stay positive, she imagined her own animated magical transformation sequence. Lengths of gold ribbon shooting across tasteful shots of her body, boots and gloves flying onto her hands and feet, followed by the short shorts and top materializing in a shimmer of silver energy. Doves flying in the background. The perfect pose upon finishing, with a wink to the camera. A row of effeminately handsome men in tuxedos, weeping at the beauty and grace of what they saw before them. Yes. This.

"Oh, what do you even do?" she said to her bra, tossing it into a far corner of the room.

Kendra, no longer having pockets, grabbed an old purse her mother had lent her, its black, mottled skin looking out of place beside her white and silver costume. Going into the bathroom, she removed a cluster of hair clips before pulling everything back into a pony tail like Erica Elastic's. Kendra used the narrowness of the bathroom mirror to pretend someone else was putting her headband on for her, a personal attendant in some royal court she oversaw.

"Okay lady, deep end of the pool."

Coming down a flight of stairs, Kendra looked across the main convention floor. Movies, television shows, video games, board & role-playing games, books, and even some tech companies were all represented on their own, often overlapping, turf out on the floor. Being Kendra's first convention, it was all she knew. However, not long ago she wouldn't have found large movie studios showing off their next blockbuster in the same convention as small press science fiction authors or app developers hawking their latest wares around the corner from table-top war gamers battling across detailed styrofoam landscapes. Over time they had all amalgamated in an attempt to share each other's audiences, like baby animals clustering together to share body heat. Media Consumption Con was a product of the recession as much as the recognition of nerd culture's profitability.

Paul spotted Kendra and waved his staff at her. She waved back and came down to meet the guys by the game supplies booth where they'd clustered.

"Your costume looks truly stunning." Paul told her.

"Yeah, it's pretty cool." Richard agreed, Tim nodding as he did.

"Ah," Kendra looked down, away from their welcome comments, then pulled a glossy con schedule out of her purse, "It's alright. So okay, I think we agreed to start with the webcomic booths. What are we doing after, again?"

"Uh…" Paul flipped open an old hotel bible whose cover he'd painted black, then detailed with red symbols of a half dozen evil cults he'd invented, con schedule pages nestled inside, "We were going to try to get into the Hieroglyph Studios room to see the actor's panel for Space Elevator."

"I heard they're gonna show some scenes from the movie." Said Richard.

"That panel's gonna be awesome." Tim said.

"Yeah, if you like line-ups." Kendra replied, "Plus anything they show is gonna be online before bedtime. You guys can do that, I want to see Eliza Scotchwater talk and maybe get my copy of her new book signed."

"Okay. Before we start, I need to," Paul closed his prop bible, sighed, "use the washroom. Ugh."

"What?" Kendra asked.

"They. Are. So. Disgusting." Paul answered, nearly taking someone's eye out with his staff as he stepped aside to let another group pass by.

"Haha, boys. You so gross." Kendra reached into her purse, "Here, the clerk thought my dad was staying with me, so she gave us two keys. You can take one and use my bathroom for the day, if it makes you feel better."

Paul took the navy blue plastic keycard. "Very."

An hour later, after agreeing on when and where to meet later, Kendra said goodbye to the guys. Finding a folding chair near to the stage where Eliza Scotchwater was due to appear in five minutes, Kendra sat down with a shopping bag full of webcomic merch, only to see two better seats, dead center in the front row, being abandoned by stragglers from the last author's talk. Kendra has barely begun to stand before a couple, holding hands, took her prize. Dropping back onto her seat, Kendra was joined by a younger girl. She was looking just past Kendra, to the front row.

"Oh, you wanted one of those seats too, huh?"

"Yeah." Answered the girl beside her. Kendra looked back at the couple.

"The worst part is, you can tell his girlfriend doesn't want to be here, but probably insisted on coming." Kendra said, "It's like, if you can't tell the difference between a skill and an attribute or don't understand why the comics have a guy Thor and a lady Thor, then let your fella off his leash already."

"M-maybe she wants to be here? Or he dragged her here?"

"Hmmmmm…no. Look at the fashion shit she has on. Look at how she keeps adjusting his hair and clothes. Total helicopter girlfriend."

This girl beside her, rounded tops of long ears pointing out between curtains of straw blond hair, didn't seem to know what to say. She wrinkled her round little nose, then changed the topic of conversation.

"I really like your Erica Elastic costume."

"Oh! Thanks. I'm Kendra, by the way."

"I knew it! I'm Celine." Celine, wearing pink, fuzzy dinosaur gloves, reached out to shake hands. The glint of the zipper teeth on the dinosaur matched the reflection of the light off her braces. Charmed by the gesture, Kendra firmly shook back.

"Sorry I didn't recognize you right away, your hair looks so different." Celine explained.

"No problem, yours looks the same so I don't know what my problem is."

"Ha ha, now I'm eating your hand. Om nom nom nom." Celine giggled. Kendra laughed as the chewing of the 'dinosaur' gave her a fuzzy palm massage.

Until the moderator announced Eliza Scotchwater they killed time by agreeing the new book, Darkness Falls Over Shadowland, was her best yet and the steamy bits in chapter seven were a lot of fun to re-read. Kendra had just started to ask Celine if she was into role-playing games when the audience began clapping. Eliza was taking the stage.

For the next thirty minutes Kendra was delighted to discover

Eliza was as entertaining on stage as she was on paper, had been an awkward teenager back in the day, and she was already working on a new book starring one of Kendra's favorite characters from the shared universe within all of Scotchwater's books. Best of all, here was an adult who seemed proof positive as people get older they don't have to give up the interests of their youth or stop being fun. Kendra hoped she could be the same by the time she had grey hair, wrinkles, and a constant need for at least three layers of knitted shawls.

Finally it was time for the Q&A. Kendra had had a question burning in her for the entire talk and dozens of hands shooting into the air made it clear she wasn't alone. Celine was even making a small, urgent noise under her breath as she waved one fuzzy dinosaur glove back and forth. A convention volunteer in a blue t-shirt brought a microphone over to a woman in her thirties.

"Hello Ms. Scotchwater." The woman said, "You know, my husband wanted me to ask this question for him. He's so shy, my hubby. Anyways, my husband wanted to know…"

Kendra's sudden annoyance blocked out whatever the woman's question had been. She was very familiar with people her own age who, having just started their first relationship, would find ways to shoehorn 'my boyfriend' or 'my girlfriend' into any conversation. It drove her nuts, and not just because she hadn't had a relationship yet. There was a pronunciation, always accenting the first syllable, which got in her ear like an aural wet willy. Until now, Kendra had just assumed people left this behind after graduating high school. Discovering there were people who did the same thing with 'husband' undercut her hope people grew out of ill behavior like old baby clothes, and left her wondering what she'd be like as an adult.

This was painted over by a bright blue burst of excitement shooting up through her chest as, yes, a volunteer came toward Kendra with a microphone. Kendra asked her question about the evolving characterization of two mothers in Scotchwater's 'Heirloom' cycle of books. Scotchwater gave an enthusiastic answer, then provided exactly the addendum Kendra had hoped for.

"You must be a regular reader of my blog. Are you?"

"Yes!" Kendra answered, "I saw how you were surprised more people didn't ask questions about the relationship of the two mothers."

"Instead of focusing on their son Edward and his Grandfather, exactly. The men of the story are important, but so are the women! To say nothing of the girls, of course, like Edward's poor sister Louise!" Scotchwater pointed at Kendra, then looked to the moderator, "I like this one, she can come back every year, if she wants. Observant girls like her often grow up to become writers, you know."

Finished answering, Scotchwater gave a friendly nod to her new favorite audience member. Smiling ear to ear, Kendra handed the microphone back and sat down. She hadn't realized how badly she'd needed that.

A few more questions were asked before Celine got her wish as well. Holding the mic with both hands, she pushed past Kendra and headed right to the very front of the stage. It was clear if there hadn't been a waist-high curtained barrier, she would have put her face right up to Scotchwater's. Kendra wasn't sure what to make of this, though neither Eliza nor the volunteers seemed fazed.

"Um, um, uhmmmm." Celine began, "If you could be any kind of cake, which kind would you be?"

"Oh, I suppose I'd be a wedding cake, because I'd have so many layers to me." Scotchwater replied, to the delight of Celine and the crowd. When Celine stayed, her grip on the microphone as tight as ever, was when Scotchwater and the volunteers became a little unsure.

"Oh cool! Um, um, ummmmm." Celine looked down, her mouth moving a little too close to the mic, "That's really hot!"

A surprised laugh and a raised eyebrow were all the author could manage in reply. Celine shoved the mic at a volunteer, then ran back to her seat and rubbed her thighs with her hands. Kendra looked at her, wondering.

"I'm so glad we both got to ask questions." Celine whispered.

"Well." The moderator spoke up, "On that illuminating note, we're going to bring the Q&A to a close. Ms. Scotchwater will be moving over to the signing booth. You can buy a copy of her new book direct from the publisher's booth. Remember, no outside copies allowed."

"Whaaaaat?" Kendra said to nobody in particular, "I bought mine from a small book store and everything. Damn."

"I'm gonna go get one and line up." Celine said, "Wanna hang out later?"

Kendra did, so they checked they had each other's numbers,

Celine running off to get in line about a tenth of a second after they were done.

"Alright man, I'll take a look." There were a decent amount of people staying for the next author. Kendra couldn't tell which one of them spoke. Well, not until he made the most unsubtle one hundred and eighty degree turn in his chair she'd ever seen, looked her up and down, then turned back to talk to his friend.

"Naw, I'm not into skinny bitches." He wasn't good at whispering, either, or he didn't care to be, "You know, like that song. How's it go?"

The pedantic part of her couldn't help wanting to know which of the many recent songs he was referring to which let women know, by taking a dump on skinny girls, it was okay to be curvy. This part was outvoted by every other fiber in her being. Kendra shot up and took long strides across the convention floor, dodging bulging backpacks and swinging shopping bags as she did so. In her head Kendra, not worrying about a specific destination, made a game out of trying to create the longest straight line between her and the guy who'd just passed judgment on her figure.

"Last chance to sign up! Hurry if you want to fight for the Emperor's entertainment and maybe even win your freedom!" Mr. Gregory?

Big beard. Thick, rounded off square glasses. Healthy gut, chest, and arms all wrapped in yellow & beige plaid. Yup, it was her World Issues teacher alright, standing around a massive home-made board laid across a two by two grid of rectangular folding tables. The arena of play was made from joined-together slats of particle board, hand-painted with a top down depiction of the Roman Coliseum, and an overlay of thin black lines creating a grid of hexagons over top; a product of long hours in a garage or den, working with small pots of paint, rulers, Exacto knives, and other tools of the tabletop gaming hobbyist. Kendra put a hand to her chest as she walked up to the edge, running her eyes over every detail.

"Maybe one of my students would like to fight for Caesar's amusement?" It took a moment for Kendra to look up at this.

Checking her phone, Kendra saw she had another two hours to kill before her and the guys were to meet up again over by the video game corner of the convention floor. Mr. Gregory pulled out a large fishing gear box and opened it to reveal small, pewter, hand-painted gladiator miniatures, every bit as colorful as any fishing lure. One of them, an Ethiopian woman holding a trident and net, caught her eye.

"Hell yes!"

Taking her spot along the edge of the improvised mega-table, along with twenty-nine other participants aged eight to fifty-eight, Kendra let out a small sigh of relief. The company, the activity, where her head needed to be to play; the asexuality of it all was more refreshing than any cold drink.

For the next two hours Kendra lost herself in shifting alliances, dice rolls as tense as any found at a casino, and the short improv performances of players describing their imaginings of how each clash of numbers translated into cinematic bloodshed. Passing strangers stopped to watch the battle, often checking in on fighters they'd decided were worth following, and added to the roar of the group whenever someone was killed in a spectacular fashion or held on in the face of terrible odds.

Eventually crushed between the shields of two hulking Murmillos, Kendra ranked fifth of thirty. Having made it so far, wounding one of the swordsmen with her dying breath, she was content. Kendra thanked Mr. Gregory before heading off, thoughts of the jerk at the author Q&A now buried under a mountain of moments from the miniature massacre.

Twenty minutes later Kendra was teamed up with Richard in a co-op match of Hat Wars 3 against players at a convention in Germany, the two of them enjoying the attention of a small audience drawn in by a studio employee charged with showing off the new game. Down to two minutes left in the match, Kendra and Richard were tied with the Germans for total kills. Looking up at the ninety-inch plasma screen, they charged around a cartoonish rendering of a WWII bomb factory, each of them low on health.

Down to thirty seconds, Kendra came upon both German players in a soot smeared cul-de-sac. The ensuing firefight left her dead, but also drew the enemy into the end of a tunnel Richard was watching through the scope of his sniper rifle. Two loud cracks followed, and they won the match by a single point. The audience cheered, then jockeyed to be the next ones to play.

"See, sniping is the best!" Richard told Kendra.

"Yeah, take that Germany. You may have almost one hundred percent clean energy, but we have skills, bitches!" Kendra went for a high five and while the execution was fine, letting her arm swing back down didn't go so well. Whether it was the crush of the crowd pushing for the PC's, his occasional misreading of personal space boundaries, or a bit of both, Paul was standing close enough behind Kendra for her hand to connect with his crotch.

Tim and Richard's sympathetic sounds came so close on the heels of Paul's groan it sounded like the opening note of a terrible a capella performance. Both hands on himself, Paul staggered like a horse who'd taken on one saddlebag too many.

"Oh God, Paul, I'm so sorry!" Kendra was not ready for this.

"Ah, boy." Paul, hands welded to his groin, stumbled backward and turned so he could rest against the nearest corner of the booth. The distraction of the new Hat Wars 3 match mercifully spared him any more spectators for his pain. Kendra just stared, blushing, and wanting to be anywhere else at all.

"*Did I even hit him hard?*" she thought, *"It was more like a gentle cupping, maybe?"*

Half-reaching toward him as if to help, Kendra looked to Richard and Tim. The former shrugged, an amused grin on his face, while Tim was doing a poor job of stifling his laughter. Kendra stood up as straight as she could and turned to look for something to excuse a quick exit. Five booths down, she saw what she needed.

"Uh, okay, so there isn't anything I can do to fix this." She announced to the guys, Paul still holding himself, "I'm gonna go over on my own and check out the Dance Panic Ninety-Nine booth for a bit. I'll text when I'm done and we can meet up, okay?"

"Sure." Richard replied.

"Sorry to be making such a fuss, but, you know." Paul said. Kendra nodded, then slipped through a gap in the crowd.

As Kendra reached the Dance Panic Ninety-Nine booth, a neon-lit church dedicated to spreading the gospel of the next version of the game, DP99 Turbo Championship Edition, she wasn't surprised by the booth babe in a more professional version of her own costume. She didn't begrudge a waitress, or whatever, for trying to make some extra money on the side or for having a body closer to the unreality of most women in video games. What did surprise Kendra was the male booth babe in an Egon Electric costume. He wasn't some chunky former football player or grinning ectomorph reflecting her own figure back at her. He had the lean muscles of a gymnast, large, expressive eyes, perfect teeth, was two or three years older than her, with relaxed, friendly body language, and wearing a tight fitting, bicep-baring costume designed by a team of artists to be the perfect compliment for hers. He was, he was…

He was just the best.

Before Kendra could approach him for a photograph, someone tapped on her shoulder.

"Excuse me." A guy in his early twenties said, "Can I have my photo with you?"

Shopping bag full of merch. Thick soled sneakers for hours of standing and walking. Jeans. Loose fitting black t-shirt, with an Osamu Tezuka illustration on the chest. A little doughy in the middle, accentuated by a slouched posture. She'd never met this guy, but she knew this guy.

"Ha! I appreciate it, but I think she's who you want." Kendra pointed to the female booth babe. Tezuka shirt shook his head.

"No, no I mean you."

"Uhhhhh, sure?" Kendra tapped on her chin, "I think I know who can take the picture for us." The male booth babe had just finished having his picture taken with a couple of grinning teenage boys. Kendra walked over to him in a way she hoped was at least a little bit seductive. God, she just wanted to run her fingers along those collarbones of his. Surprising herself, she successfully flirted a bit when asking the model to take the picture. His name was Tyler.

"I'm Graham." The con-goer told them, handing his phone to Tyler. Kendra tried to do some of the more exaggerated poses she knew from Dance Panic Ninety-Nine. Graham stood with his arms by his sides. A few quick photos later and Kendra put the second part of her plan in action, asking Graham to take pictures of her with Tyler. He was happy to do so. Soon, Kendra and Tyler stood side by side to mimic the promotional art of Egon Electric and Erica Elastic printed on a ten foot banner above them.

"I like your costume, it's really good!" Tyler said.

"Oh," Kendra felt an uncomfortable, though not unwelcome, heat shift across her stomach, "you said that to the last girl who dressed like Erica Elastic."

"Nope. I just smiled and tried not to comment when her power crystal popped out."

"I hope 'power crystal' doesn't mean anything else." Did that innuendo work? She didn't care. Graham took a couple of photos while they cycled through poses, then Tyler made a suggestion: what if they did the big victory pose when the game was beaten with a perfect score?

Tyler put one hand on the back of his neck, realizing what he was suggesting, "Well, if you're okay with being hugged from behind and picked up off the ground. We can do something else if you wouldn't be comfortable, like maybe-"

"I," Kendra enunciated as clearly as she could, "would be okay with this."

"Why don't I take a short video?" Graham suggested.

"Yeah, then we can do the full animation. I like your thinking, man." Tyler said. Kendra began sending mental waves of thanks to Graham.

After two false starts, one where Kendra didn't quite move fast enough and another where Tyler almost twirled them both into the corner of the booth, Kendra enjoyed looking across the convention floor with her toes three feet off the ground. Like a carnival ride she'd buy a hundred tickets for, her point of view slowly swung around and down, Tyler shifting his grip on her hips to twirl her so she saw him, the convention, him, the convention, and then Graham as her boots connected with carpet. Eyes on the lens of her phone's camera, mind on Tyler's fingers splayed across her abdomen, Kendra knew exactly what she was going to do after this perfect point in her life was forced to end by the rude shove of linear time.

Thanking them both, Kendra took her phone back and tried not to think about how her index finger grazed Graham's. She had nothing against him, she just didn't want any interference with her thoughts of having everything against Tyler. A grid map of the convention floor opened in another window of Kendra's mind, like the board her Ethiopian net hurler had been battling on earlier. Plotting the quickest possible path back to her room, Kendra enjoyed the feeling of clearing ground with steps which were at least on a first name basis with flat-out leaping. In her head she held everything her senses had taken in of Tyler with the care of someone bringing water from a well.

Taking the stairs, not wanting to risk brushing against anybody in elevators she knew were seeing a lot of traffic, Kendra already had it all worked out.

The bathroom. She thought, taking two stairs at a time, *Hand towel on the edge of the sink so my butt doesn't get cold on that fake marble stuff. Feet braced against the door frame.*

Pushing the door open into the hallway of the hotel's fifth floor, Kendra nearly drove it into the face of a pair of twelve year old girls with their mother.

"Sorry!" Kendra called behind her, charging for her room, "Really gotta go to the bathroom!"

The next few minutes already worked out like a NASA shuttle launch, Kendra started to wonder if she could think of an excuse to get her photo taken with Tyler on the second day of the convention. She couldn't focus, digging her keycard from her mom's old purse, and decided to postpone this particular piece of problem-solving.

Door closed behind her, Kendra ran one hand across her stomach where Tyler had touched her and wondered if she could make the ten feet to the bathroom. Then again, the double bed was six feet away. If Celine came by, she could always fake being halfway through changing.

Jumping back onto the bed, Kendra began pulling down her shorts before she finished bouncing on the mattress. Eyes closed, kicking off white spandex past her boots, she abandoned her plan to watch the video and re-allocated valuable fingers to sneaking under her top. A small starburst went off behind her eyes.

Then she heard the toilet flush.

"What the fuck!" She scrabbled for her shorts where they'd landed by the bathroom door.

"Hey, don't worry, it's just me!" Paul shouted over the sound of the toilet tank refilling. He opened the bathroom door and looked down to see Kendra straightened out on the floor, just managing to get her shorts up in time, a sideways exclamation mark punctuating her own surprise. She stared back, eyes wide, face flush, hair fallen from its ponytail to tumble out across the floor, chest rising and falling.

Bolting up without thinking, Kendra once again found Paul standing a little too close. Before she could take a step back, his lips were on hers and a hand had rushed to press along her lower back. The sensation of Tyler's hand on her stomach was obliterated by the coldness of Paul's glasses bumping the bridge of her nose. Sliding out, she pushed backwards, nearly tripping over her own feet.

"Hey!" Kendra said, covering her chest.

"I wasn't looking at your breasts." Paul protested.

"There's other reasons girls do this." Kendra wished she'd worn a bra after all. Glancing over her shoulder, she saw it bunched up by the bedside table where Paul had to have seen it, "God, Paul, what the hell?"

"I'm sorry, it's just…" Paul waved one hand up and down in her direction, "And you didn't hit me hard earlier, it was more like you cupped me."

I knew it! Kendra thought.

He explained he'd been overacting earlier, to cover up "a partial…reaction", how no girl ever touched him there, and he'd given up on the idea anyone ever would.

"Oh, Paul." Kendra let her arms go down, "That's so sad. You shouldn't think that. Somebody'll fuck you I'm sure."

"Do you have to be so crude? Why are you like this now?" Paul put his hands on his hips, "Did something untoward happen between you and Will Daniels?"

Kendra thought about how it had only been a few weeks since she'd stored up those kisses with him in the woods. Now Paul's lips had painted over those. She turned to the window, then back to her friend.

"I knew it. People were talking." Paul said, "All this time I've…and you haven't even noticed."

"Geez Paul, what do I say? I mean, this is pretty out of the blue." It was to her, she'd gotten so used to thinking of Paul and the guys as safe, sexless friends of early childhood, she'd never seen the subtle clues to Paul's growing affections, "Aren't you're always staring at Val? She even has a name for how distracted you get, Eh-Double-Dee, like A.D.D.?"

"Oh." Paul started hard at the floor, as if Kendra was still laying there in front of him, "That doesn't matter. I like you. You're the one I've known forever. You're the only girl I know who likes to do so many of the same things I do, who I can talk about them with."

"What about some of the girls at this convention?" Kendra said, "They're not all from out of town."

"I don't know them." He answered, looking back up with moist eyes, "How would I introduce myself? What would I, I mean, how do you even…?"

Kendra opened and closed her mouth three times, then gave up.

"I," Paul looked at the floor, "I have feelings for you."

Mind reeling, Kendra joined him in admiring the carpet; a pair of detectives examining the chalk outline of their friendship.

A group of laughing kids passed through the hallway outside the room.

"Can't you just," Kendra tried to think, couldn't, "not?"

"What?"

"I dunno, I'm sorry, I'm the worst."

"Kendra, it isn't just feelings of…love." They both were startled by the word as it hit their ears. Paul pressed on, "You don't understand what it's like to be a guy. All the time, all the time, there's this nagging…"

"Paul, I get it. I want sex all the time too, but…"

"So why don't we help each other?" Paul stepped over and reached to touch her. She pulled away, his fingers never connecting.

"Paul, no!"

"It's bullshit!" Paul turned his back to her, "Women want sex so much less then men do, always, always, always."

"Paul, please leave." Kendra replied, "Maybe we can talk later, but, yeah."

Paul stamped his way to the door, tossing her spare keycard behind him. "We are such a poorly designed species!"

SLAM

"Hello? Kendra, are you in there?" She raised her head at the sound of a familiar dialect of braces. It was Celine. Sliding off of the bed, Kendra went to greet her at the door.

"Hey."

"Hey! You weren't answering your phone so I thought maybe it'd died and I just came here." Celine asked. One text from Richard, asking what had happened to Paul, and Kendra had pulled out the battery. In the two hours since then she'd mostly tried to escape everything by falling asleep, with mixed results.

"Uh," Kendra thought about it, "Yeah, sure." It wasn't Celine she felt too embarrassed to be seen by. She took a cursory glance down either end of the hall. It was clear.

"Why aren't you in your costume anymore?"

"Oh," Kendra looked down at the old air show sweater, brown cords, and black converse she'd changed into after Paul left, "I got cold, I guess."

"Well, I think you were really brave to wear it. I wouldn't have had it in me." Celine said, "Listen, I'm gonna get pad thai from that booth near the entrance. Do you want to come?"

"What time is it?"

"Like, six-thirty."

Kendra remembered the guys would be taking part in a big, ten person D&D dungeon crawl with prizes for whomever survived. She was supposed to be there with them.

"Are you okay?" Celine asked, "You look a little sour."

Stepping out into the hall and closing the door, she replied "That's because I just had to swallow a big dose of my own medicine."

PART THREE

I Don't Mean to Alarm You

Two years after Paul startled her in a hotel room, Kendra scoured the menu for something which wouldn't cost more than she had in her pocket, after tipping. Trying to ignore the modern music which didn't match the mood of the retro nineties imitation fifties diner she was meeting Gwen in, Kendra made her choice and laid the menu down so it lined up with the corner of the table.

"Oh, uh, I'm still waiting for my friend." She told the waiter when he came by. Gwen wasn't her friend, though, and hadn't been for about two years. Kendra assumed they'd never hang out again, drifting away from each other's lives after they graduated in three weeks time. However, cheap diner food wouldn't pay for itself, so here she was.

Now there was Gwen, coming through the glass double doors as if she were stepping on stage. Kendra couldn't remember if this had started before Gwen became tangled up with the drama kids or if she'd always done it. The top half of a grey unitard flowed up from high waisted jean shorts with pockets poking out the ragged bottoms of its legs let Kendra know Gwen must have been coming from school, or at least somewhere she could change out of whatever uniform her parents had assigned that day. Reaching into her transparent plastic backpack, Kendra pulled out Gwen's phone and reviewed her work as she waited for its owner to finish approaching the table.

It pleased Kendra to have more control over these devices needed for membership in the human race. She'd meant to learn how to root phones for a while, finding motivation after tripping over an ancient online article about the Apple 4S version of Siri telling a user in Manhattan it was unaware of any nearby abortion clinics when there'd been several. From there she'd looked up others, like the one about how the parental control filter on iOS 12 blocked "how to say no to sex" but allowed searches like "how to make a bomb". Many summer evenings of online research and weeks of practice later, Kendra had spent the school year making extra income by charging other students for removing parental monitoring software from their phones. No more burner jobs for her.

"Hey Kendra!" Gwen sat across from Kendra, "I like your hair! What color is that?"

"International Orange, Aerospace." Kendra answered, looking aside for a moment, "I think it's #ff4f0…0?"

"Uh, yeah, sounds right." Gwen tapped her finger on the table, "Can I have my phone?"

"Sure. Can I have my forty dollars?"

Kendra put the money in her trusty duct tape wallet. As she did so, Gwen spotted a curious bill.

"Oh cool, is that foreign money?" She asked, taking the slip of paper without waiting for permission.

"It's something Camilla gave me. Her older sister, Paola,

brought it from L.A."

It was a Mexican one thousand peso bill transformed into an art project, keeping only its original overlapping grid of pinks and purples. The face of Miguel Hidalgo y Costilla was replaced with the head and shoulders of Sailor Moon, alongside the golden crescent within a winged heart that was so much a part of the magical girl's personal brand. The value had been changed to six hundred and sixty-six.

"What is it? Like, what's it from?" Gwen asked.

"Honestly, I don't know. I started to look it up, then decided I prefer the mystery." Kendra pinched the bill between two fingers, pulling it from Gwen's hand, and returned it to her wallet.

"So you and Camilla are friends now? But isn't she close with-"

The waiter came, saw Kendra's wallet out, and tried to make a joke of how he didn't mind if they paid first so long as they tipped well. The girls each gave him the same practiced, polite smile before ordering. Gwen asked for a cheeseburger with fries and a coke. Kendra ordered a chicken sandwich with sweet potato fries. Gwen changed her side to a salad. Kendra changed her side to a salad. Gwen changed her cheeseburger to a veggie burger and her coke to a bottle of water. Kendra snorted, then changed her order to "The greasiest Philly Cheese Steak you've got, with lots of fries and a large chocolate milkshake.", shooing the waiter away before Gwen could say anything.

"Well, I guess you run track." Gwen said.

"I kinda stopped just before the end of last summer." Kendra replied, leaning back in her seat, "It's not like I'll ever be good enough to go pro. Plus I got tired of seeing Mary and Kevin so much."

They sat quietly until the waiter brought their drinks, then a little longer still. Kendra, having thought Gwen was as eager to be anywhere else as she was, began to wonder.

"Hey Kendra."

"Hey Gwen."

"What's it say on your shirt? I can't figure it out."

Kendra obliged, opening her brown corduroy blazer to fully reveal the bold white text on her black V-neck. It read

NESSIE &

SASQUATCH &

CHUPACABRA &

MISANDRY

"I got the idea from looking at one of my Dad's old shirts." Kendra explained, "His had the names of The Beatles on it."

Their meals arrived. Kendra didn't want to eat much, still being a little full from breakfast. Spite helped Kendra push large mouthfuls of meat, bread and cheese past her lips while Gwen nudged her salad around with a fork.

"Mmmm." Kendra said, "So how's theater?"

"Oh." Gwen looked away, "I think I've grown out of it."

"How you do even-" Kendra realized something, "Do you still hang with the friends you made?"

"I think I've outgrown them too." Gwen took a bite of her sandwich. Kendra laughed, startling Gwen.

"Well then I guess you've really outgrown me, 'cuz we met way before."

"Oh no! No, not at all." Gwen put both hands on the table, as if to steady herself, and looked Kendra right in the eye, "I mean, yeah I've known you longer, but you keep changing."

"What."

"Kendra, you're not who you were when we hung out last time. You're more confident. Most people don't make fun of you anymore. You don't take crap from boys. Heck, I heard you kissed Will Daniels even though he has a girlfriend."

"Guh." Kendra rolled her eyes, "Does it even count when they've been long distance twice the time they both lived here?"

"I know!" Gwen was happy to have something to agree on, "Anyways, yeah, you also got smart with phones."

"I was always smart."

"Of course! You didn't always dress this way, though, and that's big. The suits were…well, your own thing, and this year you've even upgraded on those."

"I guess." Kendra looked down at her brown dress pants with beige pinstripes, hemmed at the knees, worn over shiny gold leggings stopping. She ate some more sandwich, forcing Gwen to keep talking.

"This whole…style of yours, is really something. I swear Owen is totally stealing it, in a boy's way." Gwen tried for a look of friendly conspiracy; it felt off-model, "What's that about, do you think?"

Kendra frowned. It was true, Owen must have discovered similar corners of the Internet to where Kendra had been finding style ideas for the past year. Ever since he slimmed down and found 'his' new look, doing things like dying his hair aquamarine or wearing old tuxedos to school, Owen had earned a reputation as a real ladies' man. One girl was even caught lying about sleeping with him, having bragged in earshot of someone who actually had. Kendra hadn't so much as held a boy's hand since the disaster with Paul. None of this might have bothered her if she'd made her revised virginity loss deadline of turning eighteen, or if she felt confidant about meeting her latest deadline: the morning after prom. She still didn't have a date. Her frown deepened.

"Sorry, we don't have to talk about Owen." Gwen said, "Or shouldn't I have mentioned Will?"

"Oh," Kendra forced her features into something more pleasant, "No it's just, ah, who cares? Who gives a shit?"

"Yeah." Gwen gave her best false laugh, "Who gives a shit? This is nice. We should hang out more."

Popping the last of her sandwich into her mouth, Kendra thought it over. Given some changes in her social scene over the past year, it was tempting.

"No, I don't think so."

"What?"

"Gwen. Wait, just a second." Kendra shoved a greedy handful of fries into her mouth, barely chewing them, "I don't mean to alarm you, but you kind of suck?"

Ray Cats

The heat death of the universe was near. Kendrella had never been colder. Cradled in a survival pod, her friendly machine, she watched the stars. They'd once been uncountable, rough-cut gemstones spread across a bed of smooth velvet. Now, this close to the end of entropy's work, they were the last few fireflies floating through a night without end. The razor thin canopy of the pod had a frisson of frost around the edges. She pushed back harder into her oval bed of orange fur; scavenged from a wrecked pleasure cruiser that hadn't put a smile on anyone's face since before the last yellow sun turned red. It had been tempting to take the larger craft for herself, except she'd never be able to keep it fueled. Warmth and light were in short supply. Love was even harder to fine.

Bred in a tube as the final gasp of some ancient homo sapiens supremacist group's automated cloning facility, Kendrella was quite possibly the last of her kind in the entirety of existence. Any other life forms descended of man had long since moved on to become beings of pure light, uploaded consciousnesses in nanotech hiveminds, or the rarest of the rare, homo cosmos. If there were any aliens at all, they'd managed to keep out of sight of humanity and its many evolutionary offspring.

She was only "possibly" the last homo sapiens because she wasn't sure what had happened to Willenium, the one true man she'd ever known. After spending some time with her, he'd preferred to chase a woman whom he could never touch. Kendrella hadn't been able to bare her soft flesh being rejected for light projections of a 'woman' who hadn't been corporeal for over sixteen epochs. He didn't even look when she took her then-fully-stocked survival pod from the bay of his hunting ship and set to fleeing as far away from his face as she could. She'd find a new face to lay over his, a new human of any gender, anyone with whom -

*

"Any gender, eh?" Val asked.

"It's the far, far future and she's lonely and horny and shut up."

"I wasn't saying there's anything wrong with it. I'm just curious how this applies to you, 'Kendrella'."

*

anyone with whom -

*

"Val?"

"Kendra?"

"Please stop sitting on my back."

Val shifted from where she had straddled Kendra's shoulder-blades, pinning her to the floor. Kendra snatched the crumpled sheets of paper containing her story, her friend letting them go without protest.

"You know, if you hadn't printed these out then I never would have seen them."

"Right?" Kendra stuffed the papers deep inside her bright red bookshelf, "But it's much easier to edit on hard copy, so."

"Okay, what should I be taking from your auto-bio fan-fiction?"

Kendra ran one hand through her hair and huffed. "Take whatever you want, I don't care."

"Sorry."

"Nah," Kendra turned to look down at her friend, who was still sitting on the floor, "I could just use a break from thinking about…you know."

"Okay," Valerie knew Kendra didn't mean the heat-death of the universe, "Hey remember when we were young, with our candy stashed in the big play-structure's secret hiding space?"

"Yeah!" Kendra said, "It was that weird panel under the… yeah, I totally remember."

"Wanna go see if anybody put anything in there since we left?" Val stood up, adjusting her pale yellow blouse.

"Sure. We should get Nat to meet us." Kendra opened her bedroom door and stepped around the trio of excited sausage dogs leaping to greet her. Val followed, scooping up Salvador Doggy to carry him down the stairs into the living room, "I owe her a few bucks and she's been texting me like crazy about it."

"She's so lucky it's legal now. I don't know what she what business she could have gone into before."

"Yeah, I wonder what'll be like when she's old enough to open her own dispensary." Kendra struggled with her faded pair of black Converse sneakers. Her mother spotted them from the kitchen, where she was frying a pair of grilled cheese sandwiches, and asked what they were up to.

"Going to our old school, Mrs. Washington, for nostalgia." Val said, "We were just remembering when we were young."

Kendra's mother laughed, running a finger along the start of some grey at her temples. "You're young now, idiots."

"Uh, time's relative mom. We're talking about, like, half our lifetime's ago." Kendra said, "So to us that's 'young', idiot."

"Time's relative to my boot up your skinny ass," Her mom let out another, small laugh, "Don't come home too late and maybe…don't come home too high, please?"

"I'll watch her, Mrs. Washington." Val put both hands behind her back and gave her best class picture day smile.

"Watch me get super fuckin' baked." Kendra stage-whispered, stepping out the door with one foot and pushing back an excited Spicy Italian with the other.

Damp air. Magenta-tinged skies. Pores in concrete. Dry grass wicking moisture from their shoes. Rain had been and would soon return. Val and Kendra decided to chance it. Their old grade school, Woodenmeyer Bi-Centennial, wasn't far, it just felt that way. They hadn't wanted or needed to go there since the morning they graduated.

Reddish brown bricks and large, rectangular windows held up a faded black rooftop. The building zigged and zagged across the school-yard, having sprawled out in rushed growth spurts, each coming long after a corresponding increase in the surrounding community. When Val and Kendra had attended, there had been over a dozen portables. Now beige aluminum siding was replaced by still more reddish brown brick.

"I wonder how long before they start building on the soccer field." Kendra called out to Val, who had run ahead to grab a swing on the play structure.

"I dunno. They're definitely running out of room, huh?" Val's legs began pumping, her verdant green dress dragging on the sand underneath.

Kendra closed her eyes and took a deep breath. Due to a fortuitous fault line between school districts, most of the kids who'd tormented her in grade school had gone to a different high school. It had been a blessed escape, even if some new jerks, and her romantic frustrations, had stepped up. She'd begun to learn the dangers of nostalgia, yet still…

"Hey Val, remember when Mrs. Campbell got so mad she threw a textbook at Paul?"

Her friend laughed. "Yeah. He wouldn't shut up, even though he obviously didn't know the answer. What class was that?"

"Sex Ed."

Val laughed even harder. "Remember how they got rid of all the games on the computers except poker and blackjack? So we all became really good, what we thought was really good anyways, and brought decks to the schoolyard?"

Kendra walked over to the orange plastic slide and tried to run up to the top. She nearly made it, then stumbled back into the surrounding sand pit. "Yeah, those candies we used for poker chips were so bad as actual candy."

"Rockets! Purples were the most valuable." Val launched herself, landed, and went right back to the swing. "Hey, you just gonna watch me?"

Kendra stopped eying the other slide, which resembled a long, narrow baking tray and whose metal surface had, in warmer weather, burned more than one set of buns. She hung her light grey corduroy jacket on the nearest play-structure post, revealing tall portraits printed on either side of a black v-neck. The front portrait was in black and white, showing Margaret Hamilton, big glasses and a bigger smile, beaming with pride while placing the last of seventeen bound stacks of paper, any of which could give the Tokyo phone directory feelings of inadequacy, on top of a pile as tall as she was. Underneath her portrait, in digital clock font, it read SOFTWARE. On the back was Linda Hamilton in Terminator 2, with an AK-47, attitude for days, and, beneath her in bold impact font, HARDWARE.

Between the pricey transfer paper for her dad's printer and a few messed up prototypes, this had cost Kendra three times what she would have paid to have the shirt done by a professional print shop. She felt learning a knew skill was worth it.

Kendra took the swing beside her friend and pushed off. Feet kicking high above their heads, the girls swung to and fro, close enough to talk and never quite in sync. Kendra admired the light grey of her corduroy pants when they were up against the sky, with its gradient wash from amethyst to eggshell blue. Loose strands of Popsicle-orange hair came free, falling in and out of her view.

"Hey Val, can I tell you something kind of weird?"

"Of course."

"I'd kind of like to figure out a degree, and then a career, combining international aid, psychology, and sex therapy all together." Kendra was glad they had something to keep them looking forward, away from each other, "Maybe even solve problems with sex, like those sexual surrogates or what Ilona Staller tried to do."

"Uh huh." Val knew better than to guess at the unfamiliar name, "Who'd you read about now?"

Kendra explained at length how Ilona Staller had been a pornstar turned member of Italian Parliament, how she'd offered to have sex with Saddam Hussein in exchange for peace during the first Gulf war and had renewed her offer when he'd refused to let America see the weapons of mass destruction he didn't have. She wasn't sure why Staller had waited until two thousand and six to make a similar offer to Osama Bin Laden, "But imagine if he'd taken her up on it!"

"I'm not sure what-"

"I mean, jerkoff had a mountain of porn in his bedroom where he died, so you know sexual frustration was the foundation of all his horseshit."

Val listened to her friend's voice wind down into a mumble, Kendra's embarrassment at her rising emotion pressing down on the volume button. When Kendra eventually went all the way to zero, Val spoke.

"It would be nice if sex could actually solve problems like that."

"It solves a lot more than that. Sex helps with your immune system, bladder control, blood pressure, it counts as exercise, improves sleep, eases stress, stimulates production of a natural anti-depressant…"

"Okay, but sex doesn't solve things in general, other than not having sex, and can totally lead to new problems."

"Well, how would you know?" Kendra tried not to sound bitchy. She knew Val was just thinking out loud.

"I…wouldn't, I guess. But I mean, I read, I watch shows, and hear what other people say."

"Yeah, we observe, we get impressions. It's not the same as doing." She kicked out, white laces whipping around, "Meanwhile, everybody else gets to live longer, learning all kinds of - whoah!"

Kendra went so high she almost achieved a childhood dream of flipping around and over the bar. Alarmed, she went stiff and swung back down to bang her heels on sand packed hard by hundreds of feet who'd come before her. Head jostling, chains bending to pinch skin along the inside of her clenched fists, it took Kendra a second to focus her vision.

"Ah geez."

"You okay, K?"

Kendra just nodded in the direction of the other side of the playground. Coming through a gap in the chain-link fence around the field were a group of girls she hadn't seen in years, all heading their way. Kendra figured they must have been playing soccer in a nearby field, what with the uniforms they wore; black shorts, cleats, white shirts with numbers on the back and the cartoon head of a ferocious cheetah high on the left side of the chest. There were seven of them, blood up and hair down.

"Magnificent." Kendra spat.

"D'you wanna go?" Val slid to a stop.

"No. We have every right to be on these swings."

"Sure. Doesn't mean we have to take their shit."

"I'll just deal with it like I always did." Kendra sat upright, squaring her shoulders, "Show those bitches who's boss, like I used to."

"Uh, Kendra?" Valerie whispered while looking at her friend, the approaching girls taking up more and more of her peripheral vision, "Usually it was me who-"

"Hey Val, Kendra. Long time no see."

Val kept looking at Kendra, who stared at the speaker; a bruiser with powerful thighs, lithe arms, and piercing green eyes beneath a forehead looking like it could bounce a fist as easily as a soccer ball. Jet black hair, freed from a red scrunchie now resting on her right wrist, glistened with sweat. Charlotte preferred to go by 'Charlie', calling others any damn thing she pleased - especially if they struck her as an easy target.

"Hey Charlie. Jamie. Steph. Emily. Jenn. Lindsay. Meg." Val tried to come off cool, which wasn't easy with her butt squished into half a loop of vulcanized rubber hanging by two chains.

"Boring." Kendra replied.

"What?" Charlie said.

"'Long time no see.'? Jesus."

Charlie paused, then gave a big smile as she turned to her teammates. "Hey guys? Remember when Kendra cried 'cause she dropped her porno book in a puddle?"

It had been a copy of Fanny Hill ten year old Kendra had been struggling with and it hadn't been dropped so much as taken from her hands before being slam dunked, by Charlie, into a mud puddle known for giving all-day soakers. Kendra chewed the inside of her lip, trapping her tongue, wanting but not wanting to remind everyone what really happened. It wouldn't help. Words wouldn't help. Words were all she had.

"You still reading porno? Probably. You a virgin?" Charlie stuck her chin out at her target, "Definitely."

Kendra shot up so her tormentor wouldn't be literally looking down on her. Charlie feigned fear for her friends amusement.

"You know, pagan moon priestesses used 'virgin' to mean a sexually independent woman, right? Sleeping with whomever she chose, not 'needing' anybody. It wasn't until later Christian translators couldn't stand the idea of the Virgin Mary having sexual…" Kendra twirled her right hand, trying to remember a word from her private studying, "…agency. So they decided 'virgin' meant someone who'd never had sex at all. Someone meek and 'pure' and pliable."

From feigned fear to confusion to amusement, Charlie's features took a trip while Kendra lectured.

"Thanks for the info, Wikipedia Brown. Any of that help solve the mystery of why the boys don't call?" Charlie's audience laughed, some of them taking a step closer to Kendra.

"I'm just trying to teach you something."

"How about I teach you something?" Charlie got close enough for Kendra to smell the Gatorade on her breath.

"Women shouldn't be fighting each other, Charlotte, we should-"

"Oh so now you're telling me what to do?" Charlie's puffing herself up, trying to excuse the violence she wanted to inflict with a pantomime for her peers, wasn't convincing anyone. Charlie wasn't angry, she was bored. It didn't make any difference to her teammates who, showing the instinctual cooperation helping them clean up on the field that season, assumed positions for blocking Kendra if she tried to run.

"How about I just do what I want?" Charlie said, reaching to take the neck of Kendra's shirt in her hand.

Val, forgotten by everyone, drew in a deep breath. "How about I fuck your dad?"

Charlie turned to look down at Val, still sitting in her swing, ankles crossed and eyes staring straight back through a slim gap in the circle of girls around Kendra.

"I can kick your ass too." Charlie offered.

"Cool, I'll say your Dad gave me the bruises when I broke him in your bedroom like the bad-boy bronco I bet he is."

Kendra just stared at her friend. She wanted to re-word Val's threat so it wasn't mangled by overreaching for alliteration. She wanted to give her a huge hug for stepping in. She wanted to grab Val's arm and escape Charlie and her squad, somehow. She wanted to stop hearing the beat of her own heart.

"Bitch, you listen." Charlie's anger pantomime had become

calmer and more convincing, "My dad loves my mom. Would he ever do anything with you? No. So cut it out."

"You 'member how I used to deliver ad flyers on your street? Your dad looked at me then, when I was just twelve." Val arced her back slightly, "Think if I came by once a week now, he'd do more than look? Think he'd be able to hold out? Week after week after week…"

"You, you dumb…" Charlie's voice quivered, "Well, how 'bout I screw your dad, huh?"

"He is dead." Val over-enunciated, "Charlotte." A long stretch of silence followed, everyone waiting for the space between Val and Charlie's eyes to burst aflame.

"Good!" Charlie yelled at the top of her lungs, a thin sliver of spittle clinging to her lower lip.

Val just stared, the rise and fall of her chest betraying how much effort it was taking to stay still. Charlie spun around and slapped Kendra's sunglasses right off her face.

"Hey!" Val stood up.

"My mom's gonna put some sausages on the barbecue. Let's go." Charlie beckoned her entourage to follow as she walked back to the gate they'd come through, not looking back at Kendra or Val even once. Val watched them leave, Kendra keeping an expression of awe pointed at her friend even while bending for her sunglasses.

"Shit, Val."

"Hey, you get all these people telling you your body is a dangerous distraction for men, 'cause they're all dumb animals who can't control their desires, or so we're told." Val crossed her arms, "You might as well leverage that bull to get out of a tough situation."

Kendra's eyes sparkled, "So you *do* listen to me when I go on my rants?"

"Of course. I always have, just like I've always backed you up with bitches like Charlie." Val poked her head up and to the left, "Huh, speaking of stuff that always happened in grade school." Her sister Natalie slouched out from behind the main body of the play-structure, hands slung deep in the pouch of her black hoodie.

Turning to pick her jacket back up, Kendra also noticed Val's sister. "Nat! You were just watching?"

"What? Three on seven isn't gonna go much better than two on seven," She shrugged, coming over to the swings, and pulled three joints out, "I'm a smoker, not a fighter."

Kendra retrieved some crumpled bills from her jacket's inner pocket, pushing them into Nat's outstretched hand.

"Hey Val," Nat continued, "Mom's friend Christina called. She says she'll take you on as an apprentice."

"Doesn't she run…uh…you know, the gender neutral clothing store downtown, in the market?" Kendra asked.

"Yeah, Agender Agenda." Val answered, a smile spreading across her face, "I'll still want to do some courses at the polytechnic and study online, but with her references and teaching I should be able to start my own custom clothing business some day."

Kendra gave in to one of her earlier desires, hugging Valory. The two held each other as Nat sparked her navy blue, Bic disposable.

"Good work, sis." Nat said, puffing away.

"I guess we should call it a night, huh?" Val said to Kendra

"Yeah." Kendra admitted, wanting to stay out later; knowing she should at least try to appease her mother.

"Hey," Val paused, "weren't we gonna check our old hiding place?"

Kendra stumbled into her room and pulled out the pages she'd snatched from Valory several hours ago. The action figure they'd found in the playstructure solved the problem of how a new character was going to look. Listening to the white noise of steady rain, eyes red, pen black, she returned to writing her story.

*

…anyone with whom she could build a lifetime of happy moments together, each experience another brick in the tomb where she'd bury all memory of Willenium and his stupid, beautiful face.

Having taught her ship to communicate by massage, a gentle rubbing of her stomach told Kendrella there was a potential fuel source nearby. Kneading the control panel, she brought golden shimmers of data up along the inside of the canopy. There was a small moon, long since abandoned by whichever planet it once orbited, and somewhere not too deep beneath its Galactic North was an intense source of energy the likes of which neither her nor the ship had ever seen. Whether this energy source was related to the moon's having a breathable atmosphere, they couldn't tell.

The pod's radiation sensors were very sensitive, but had terrible range. Kendrella could already be terminally irradiated by the time she was close enough to be told her DNA had been turned all topsy turvy. Luckily, she had the right recipe for a workaround.

The pod's modest cloning tank couldn't make anything as large as a lover for Kendrella, however it was just the right size for what she needed to safely explore the area around the energy source. Stroking a patch of white fur nine times side to side, then seven times up and down, our star-faring beauty activated the bubbling, boiling tank and set it to task. By the time the pod landed, she'd have a full complement of kitties to clear a path.

The exact origin of the Ray Cat was shrouded in mystery and splintered by apocryphal tellings of what few truths were still remembered. Given the endless mutability of language and symbol through time, past peoples had struggled to come up with a sure way of warning future generations to the presence of dangerous nuclear waste and other hazardous materials produced by their now primitive energy plants. Even the skull and crossbones had started as a symbol of rebirth, not death. Only culture and story were deemed able to survive a voyage across time and still keep some or all of the original meaning intact; and if there was one vessel for myth whom mankind had been fascinated by for the entirety of their existence, it was the feline. Thus, the Ray

Cats were bred, alongside stories and legends revolving around a very simple idea - if a Ray Cat's fur darkens, it's best to run the other way.

Even Kendrella, awoken from a larger cloning tank on a far away world with no other people around, felt a brief chill as memories of her earliest days washed over her. Dripping gel while using her unsteady legs to walk like a newborn deer, a tightly wound ball of implanted memories had already begun to unfurl within our hero's mind. During the first week of her consciousness, more than a few loosened threads had been hooked around the claw of a cautionary Ray Cat tale.

Looking through the pod's canopy with a pair of bejeweled opera glasses she'd taken from the pleasure cruiser, Kendra watched the seven white Ray Cats. Knowing what willful, difficult creatures they were, she'd had the ship brew up some cat nip and, while descending, launch it in the direction of the energy source. Spotting one Ray Cat who insisted on cleaning itself a few feet from the pod, Kendrella took a long puff from her heron-bone cigarette holder and the glowing embers of human nip at its end. Oh well, the other six were heading in the right direction. After a few minutes, the darkest color any of them had turned was an eggshell blue; nothing the human body couldn't handle.

Kendrella suited up in a chitinous jumpsuit of transparent titanium and solar panels, the latter providing power for the spider-web of exo-skeleton allowing her to move. The jumpsuit collar sent up a one-way mirrored dome of clear energy shielding, for protection and to provide the option of revealing her stunning features for any who might be deemed worthy. From afar she would look like a beautiful, nude, headless woman's body. There was no better way to disarm and distract the more dangerous creatures she might encounter.

This most lifelike of mannequins stepped from the pod to inspect the Ray Cats, weaving between the shadows of tall granite boulders scattered across the moonscape. One by one she picked up the cats and scrutinized them for subtle spots of darker tints. Protesting, each feline stared into a fish-eye lens reflection of their own features while Kendrella inspected their sensitive bellies. The cat which had turned eggshell blue deserved extra attention, hissing while its fur was pinched and pushed around. Not finding even the faintest trace of orange or, heaven forbid, black dots, she headed onward. Squeezing through a narrow gap between boulders, Kendrella was stunned by what was on the other side.

Emerging from the moon's surface at an odd angle was the opening to a tomb which could reduce any Pharaoh to envy. Once it must have towered over all of its surroundings. Now it was sunk low in the dust like the mouth of a man taking his last gasp before going under the waves for good. Light shone from a slim crack in its gargantuan doorway.

A human hand, if humans were translucent neon green, pushed up through the crack in the doorway and began to pull its owner out from below, a sonorous voice coming ahead of the rest of its owner.

"Hello? Is someone out there?" He asked, "I'm hurt. Please, have mercy."

"Don't come out yet. Who are you?" Kendrella could feel his warm tones undercutting her caution. She didn't care.

"I don't know." He replied, still just a hand to her. A strong hand with long, smooth fingers, "I hope you don't mind my saying, you sound lonely."

Kendrella bit her lip. She spoke with her suit, telling it to make her face visible and turn the jumpsuit's many surfaces into mirrors of her surroundings, flipping her from headless mannequin to floating head.

"Please, may I come out?" he asked, "Will you help me?"

"You can come out. We'll see about the rest." Kendrella changed her mind and made herself whole in his eyes, hiding nothing of herself behind mirrors. It seemed only fair, as he hid nothing of himself.

"Where are you hurt?" She asked him, "Everything…looks to be in order."

Standing a head taller than her, the green space hunk put one hand against the meat pillow of his left pectoral. On the surface, the deepness of his voice vibrated through every part of her body in the best possible way, "My heart, it aches."

Kendrella's suit told her he was the energy source. Eyes growing wide with incredulity and lust, her body told her something else. She wasn't sure about the thick wave of white hair cresting high above his neon green scalp, but the white dotted landscape where he'd shaved down the sides was about right. His shoulders spread wide, the frame from which hung a body she'd be happy to emigrate to and call her new homeland (what?). And when he turned at the sound of a Ray Cat's cry, she saw his butt was just right and oh my God Kendra just go to bed already jesus <—-—remember to cut out this bit later, seriously, it's embarrassing gah okay okay go to bed go to bed go to bed.

Dang Ol' Panda

"Hey Tim." Kendra stood outside Tim's front door with an overloaded backpack slung on one shoulder. Now she was running games herself, she had to bring more books, dice, and prepared material. All of it, even the dice, could have been condensed down into her tablet, but she felt like she spent enough time staring at glowing rectangles for everything else in her life. She was first to arrive, as usual, for the weekly Sunday afternoon gaming session.

"Hey Kendra." Tim let her into his house.

Despite everything, Kendra sometimes missed Paul's musty basement with its piles of magazines and water-damaged ceiling. It was difficult to create the right atmosphere for a game set in a cyberpunk dystopia when everyone sat in an immaculate sunroom looking out onto a perfect back yard. A floral print rug over the hardwood floor, as if the sea of flowers outside wasn't enough, bright white walls with tall oval windows, hanging family photographs in chestnut brown frames, even doilies to protect the circular wooden table they'd be gaming on; none of this screamed 'cyberpunks stealing from evil corporations, faces lit by neon signs burning through the mists of never-ending acid-rain'.

Kendra laid out her game mastering tools while Tim fiddled with his phone: Maps drawn on graph paper, pens, pencils, 4x3 cube of dice, a stack of six magazine-sized hardcover books filled with rules and fiction she'd absorbed so she could immerse the players in her own take on the world they described, and the gamemaster's screen she'd recently purchased. The screen had the usual quick-reference tables of rules on the back, the side facing the players providing a three-paneled window into a world so much worse than their own, yet so much fun to pretend to live in as some of its most marginalized citizens. It helped her feel more secure in her move from just playing, to actually running games - a move most people never made, lacking desire or confidence in their ability to create engaging, interactive worlds for their friends to have adventures in. The subtext of her replacing Paul hadn't made the transition any easier.

"You texting Richard?" Kendra asked, "Think he'll play today?"

"No." Tim put away his phone, "I was just bugging someone about this English presentation we're working on."

"Paul?" Kendra knew the answer.

"Yeah, Paul." Tim replied, "Sorry."

"It's okay, you can say his name. It doesn't bother me." *Well,* Kendra thought, *now it's been a while.*

"Okay." Tim scratched behind one ear, "I don't think Richard can make it. You wanna call him?"

"Nah," Kendra sat down in her seat, fidgeted, then got back up again, "I trust you. If he can't make it, he can't make it."

Richard hadn't been able to make it for almost a year and

Kendra hadn't seen him anywhere except school for about as long. The few times they spoke he never seemed to be quite right and she couldn't figure out why or bring herself to ask; the void of knowledge creating a chalkboard for her anxieties to diagram all kinds of horrible theories why one of her oldest, dearest friends no longer seemed to want anything to do with her. Between this and The Paul Thing, she could understand why Tim was unsure how to act when either of the guys came up in conversation. He probably knew even less than Kendra, who hadn't been keen to share all the details of what had happened in the hotel room during MediaConsumptionCon two years ago. She'd just made it clear Paul was not someone she wanted anything to do with anymore and left it at that. Had Richard said the same about her?

The doorbell went.

"I've got it!" Tim's older sister, Diana, stretched and sashayed her way from the kitchen and over to the front door. Kendra used to think she should hate Diana; for her constant exercising, her gymnast's body, clear comfort with said body, and for the way she teased Richard and Paul with it whenever they all got together for a game. Kendra was never sure if Diana was aware of the effect she had, beyond embarrassing her brother, and after a while she didn't care anymore. Diana was just too nice to hate, even if she looked like somebody a film production would call up from central casting to bully Kendra in the movie of her life.

Keeping one hand extended straight out, Diana lowered herself to grab the handle by doing the splits. The door open, Camilla watched with wide eyes as Diana slowly rose back up.

"God, Di, can't you just open the door like a normal person?" Tim said, "Why've you always gotta weird people out?"

"No, no," Camilla said, stepping inside, "I liked it.

Camilla had scaled back the Gothic Lolita look, giving her bleach-fried fringe a chance to heal, cutting a different profile without the ruffles, corsets, or bonnets, and walking around without chunky boots; leaving her a natural five foot six. She'd told Kendra it was because the girl gang thing was wearing thin, though she still spent time with her crew of cigarette-wielding Lolitas and kept in touch with Azealia. Kendra figured she was trying to make herself more appealing, but to who? Loving to flirt, she never made a move on anyone.

"Heyyyy!" Celine called, "Don't close the door!" Out of breath and wearing a rabbit-eared, heather brown, hooded onesie, Celine barged in.

"Did you think we-" Diane and Camilla spoke in unison, the latter deferring, delighted.

"Did you think we," Diane began again, "wouldn't let you in once the door was closed?"

"I dunno," Celine wheezed, pushing through toward the gaming table, "Mom was so late getting me here and I told her we didn't have time for her to finish checking her email but she was all blah blah blah and I'm so hungry and ugh." Her rabbit ears waggled back and forth, before slumping forward as she tossed her small frame in a wooden chair with a tall back. Reaching into the pouch of her onesie, she removed a worn, folded character sheet and a sack of neon green dice, then proceeded to look even more put upon when she couldn't find her favorite mechanical pencil. Two or three years the junior of everyone else in the room, Celine always managed to make herself seem even younger.

"It's so good to see you again, Diane." Camilla leaned in to give the taller girl a big hug. Head resting on Diane's shoulder, she gave a thumbs up to the gaming table. Tim rolled his eyes. Kendra gave a quick thumbs up back. Celine kept searching for her pencil.

"Nice to see you too." Tim's sister returned to the kitchen. Camilla took her seat across from Kendra, between Tim and Celine.

"Nice to see you, Tim." Camilla said, then dropped to a whisper, "Your sister is super hot."

"Dude," Tim replied, matching her whisper, "I don't like it when guys say that and I really don't know what to do when you say it."

Kendra burst out laughing when Camilla answered Tim's dilemma by giving an exaggerated shrug, coupled with a look of confusion and a vigorous jerk-off motion. Unable to help himself, Tim laughed as well. Celine's rabbit ears pointed straight to the ceiling when, curious, she brought her head up from the failed search for her pencil. Oblivious to what the fuss was about, Diana returned and held a scrubbed carrot in front of Celine's mouth.

"Hey, come on." Tim said.

"I'm not making fun of her." Diana said.

"She's not making fun of me." Celine added, sniffing the carrot, then taking it in her teeth.

"Are you dressed that way because you're a rabbit in the game?" Tim's sister asked.

"Well," Celine replied, moving the carrot so she could talk around it, "it's for me, not the game."

"Yeah, but," Kendra said, "in the game she's a hacker and, when she's in the matrix, she looks like a giant brown rabbit. All burrowing around for people's secret files. Like, 'Watership Data', right?"

"Huh." Diana turned to Tim, "Mom and I love how you've got girls coming over these days. I'd never try to drive them away."

"I've been coming over for years." Kendra said.

"Sure, but you were the only one." She replied, "Besides, I always thought you liked Richard. There's so many more possibilities now."

Kendra's face went red so fast you'd be forgiven for thinking she was a human-shaped stop sign, and the implication he might be pursuing anyone at the table sent Tim's complexion into a crimson shade of solidarity. Camilla cut in, mercifully dispelling the moment.

"Hey Kendra, is Val ever gonna join us for a game?"

"Oh yeah, uh, no." She emptied her plastic box of dice and began arranging them in a complex spiral like Busby Berkley dancers, "I've given up on getting her into role-playing games. Besides, we're getting close to the end of the campaign."

"After this, are we play-testing the next edition?" Tim asked.

"Ugh, all those new rules." Celine said, holding her carrot like a cigar, "I read some previews online and the social skill changes make, like, no sense."

"Hey guys," Diane interrupted, "how do you win these games? Do you add up points at the end of the campaign, whatever that is?"

"There's no points. You 'win' by having fun and working together to tell a cool story, I guess?" Kendra answered, "And a campaign is like a season in football or whatever, or maybe a TV show with each game being an episode building up to the finale."

"Weren't you going out?" Tim asked his sister, who put a hand to her hip and raised an eyebrow at her brother.

"Yeah, think you can hold the fort for a while? You're so under-dressed compared to your friends, I feel like they're gonna take your lunch money once I'm not around to protect you."

It was true, Tim's plain blue polo shirt and dark green cargo shorts didn't have much to say in a room with a five foot two rabbit girl, Kendra in her low-budget, best approximation of Evil Future Corporate CEO, and a Japanese-influenced Goth, even one who'd turned down her volume. Mugging for Diana, Camilla pretended to try and give Tim a wedgie. Obvious as it was she wouldn't follow through, Tim couldn't help shifting in his seat.

"Okay," Diana let out a short chuckle, "I guess you're in good hands. I left a pitcher of lemonade in the fridge for the girls. Maybe you can get them to share it with you. Dinner's at seven, so you've got plenty of time for your game."

Grabbing her small red clutch from where it hung on the antique hat rack by the door, Diana bid the gang farewell as she stepped, sauntered, and then slid out the door. As happened more and more frequently these days, especially when they ran a game somewhere dinner time didn't happen until well after Kendra thought it should, the beginning of the game became derailed by discussion of subjects closer to home than cyberware, smuggling, or stealing large amounts of Neo-Yen.

"Hey Kendra, can I buy some new stuff for my character before we start?" Celine asked.

"You still want that drone? The, uh…" Kendra flicked through one of the books she brought.

"The one with antenna that look like bunny ears," Celine clarified, "and an underbelly weapon pod."

"Hey Tim," Camilla put a hand on the table, and leaned in a little, "you know Gwen's been talking shit about you?"

"What? Why?" Tim slumped, "Why?"

"Bitch." Kendra said, brow furrowing as she hunted for the page with the stats for the drone Celine wanted.

"She's been trying to get back in with her drama pals by trading on a letter you gave her." Camilla chewed on a nail.

Kendra looked up from her book and across the table, "You did what? Tim, no…"

Camilla turned to her right, "Kendra, he asked her out to prom."

Kendra kept her eyes on Tim, "Gwen?"

"I dunno, she's cute." Tim's gaze anchored itself to a point on the table near him, "And she seemed so lonely. I remembered she used to be friends with you, so I figured she couldn't be so bad."

"But you're shy, so you asked her out with a letter." Kendra would have loved for a boy to give her a letter of affection. She didn't dare say so out loud, though, for fear Tim would go full Paul on her. *Do the not-gross guys ever get mad at the gross guys for all the opportunity their gross acts deny them?*, she wondered, *Not that I think of Tim that way, but still.*

Celine grabbed the book on drones from Kendra and began flipping through it herself. Camilla leaned back in her chair, nearly lost her balance, then settled forward with a hard clunk of six legs hitting the floor at once. Tim let out a short, soft laugh and kept his gaze rooted where it was.

"Uh, anyways," Camilla said, "If it helps, her plan didn't work. I think the drama kids laughed a little, then just turned their backs on her until she left."

"That's so like Gwen, shitting on others to try and climb a social ladder largely of her own imagining," Kendra drummed her fingers on the table, "Trying to propel herself upward like she's some kind of…of…I dunno, jerk rocket."

"Mmm, clever." Camilla sat upright, carefully.

"Oh Tim, there's got to be nicer girls out there for you." Kendra said, gesturing so it was clear these girls were Out There, not In Here. Tim flopped his head down on the table, sighing a sigh to shame all others.

"Hey Kendra, I found the drone!" Celine put a hand on her gamemaster's shoulder, "I don't have enough money. Can I roll Negotiate to get the price down?"

"Doesn't matter." Tim turned his head, keeping it on the table, "All girls go for jerks, anyways."

"Excuse me?" Kendra got up, letting both Celine's hand and her question slide away, and headed to the kitchen, "I think your theory needs a little work there, Tim."

"Yeah, I don't go for jerks." Camilla said.

"Well, but…"

"What, you don't think girls can be jerks?"

Kendra, returning with glasses of lemonade for everyone, saw Celine starting to frown.

"Tim, lift your head up and listen to me." She took her seat behind the gamemaster screen, "I'm going to revise your statement. I think instead of 'All girls go for jerks', it should read 'All girls who go for jerks, go for jerks', with the understanding that - in your definition - jerks equal People Who Are Not Tim. Right?"

"Who's Val going to prom with?" Camilla asked.

"Hey," Tim lifted his head up, "when are you gonna ask out Owen whats-his-face?"

"Why does everybody keep asking me that?" Kendra leaned back hard in both mock and real exasperation, nearly tipping herself over before waving her arms and grabbing onto the edge of the table.

"You've been awful quiet, Celine." Camilla had grown closer to the younger girl while spending the last semester tutoring her in Spanish, "What do you think? Should Kendra ask out Owen to the prom?"

"I dunno," Celine said, "Dating's weird. You know my dad has a picture of him with me in his dating profile? I guess so people think he's nice."

"Your parents divorced?" Camilla asked.

"No," Celine answered, "Mom said they're 'monogamish' and when she tried to explain it I just thought real loud about the theme song from Magical Gavin's Very Splendid Cook-Off until she stopped talking. I'm still figuring out the basics, I'm not ready for that stuff."

"Yeah," Kendra chewed her lower lip, taking advantage of the conversation to work on a map for the game, "open relationships are some next level shit."

"Figuring out the basics? I didn't get the impression you were interested." Camilla turned to Kendra, "I never see Val dating anyone, is she the same?"

Two felt rabbit paws hit the table, causing everyone's lemonade to jump.

"Guys can we play, already?" She turned to Kendra, "I mean, come on, you haven't even sent me the next chapter of 'Kendrella' yet, and if we don't play the game today then I don't know how we're going to finish the campaign before the summer is over and you guys all leave me behind to go to college and stuff."

"Kendrella?" Camilla asked the author.

"What?" Kendra deflected, then turned to Celine, "You've got a point. Sorry Celine. Also, sorry if we made you feel uncomfortable with this conversation."

"God," Celine crossed her arms, "just cause I don't talk all the time about dongs I want to sit on, doesn't mean I'm asexual. Wouldn't be bad if I was, I just hate everybody making assumptions about me. I'm dressed as a rabbit, not a dang ol'...panda!"

Celine stared at the book of drones where it lay on the table for a long moment, then remembered there was a boy at the table who heard her mention dongs and wanting to sit on them. Her face met the book at such a speed the other girls worried she'd hurt herself, then stayed there. Camilla reached over to stroke her head, pushing the ears back and letting them flop forward with each pass.

Tim wore his best poker face, but Kendra could tell he was beaming inwardly. She knew this was the kind of stuff he'd hoped he'd be privy to, lucking into regular hang-outs with a group of girls. It wasn't exactly a portal into another universe, but it wasn't the same as gaming with Richard and Paul, that's for sure.

"Okay okay, let's get down to business," Kendra gathered up her notes for the game, "This is it people, the run-up to the big finale starts now."

Yer a Problem Solver, Kendra

"I'm just having a shower!" Kendra yelled.

"I know, honey," Her Dad called from the other side of the bathroom door, "I want to know if you'd enjoy some waffles with me and your mom. I thought I should check in case you were getting brunch with Valory at that diner."

Kendra put the shower head back in its mounting. "Yeah, waffles'd be great. I'll be out in a minute. Thanks!"

A minute later, covered by three different towels, Kendra paused to look down the stairs toward the living room. A brief jolt of déjà vu gave her goosebumps. Her brother had gotten the job in construction he'd been holding out for, whatever it was, and moved out almost a year ago. While he visited whenever his laundry bag overflowed, she hadn't seen any of Greg's friends who had so freely discussed her body, tallying and sub-categorizing its sexual worth, back when she was barely into her first year of high school. She wondered if they'd been crushed by wrecking balls or falling I-beams. She wondered if the tag in Steve's shirt needed tucking in.

With college coming up in a few weeks, it wouldn't be long before Kendra left home as well. All the more reason to cut down on strip-mall diner meals and spend time with her parents at the breakfast table. She went into her room to get changed.

Kendra, trying to give herself some hips by using a metallic blue tie as a belt, slipped into a mechanic's navy blue jumpsuit. She unzipped it to the waist and rolled the cuffs back to show off her burgundy dress shirt, a brand new win from an online auction, then set to piling up her hair; now dyed a blend of cotton candy blue, ice blue, and a few strategically placed lines of white. Holding it in place with a matching cotton candy blue hair band, featuring a small bow, Kendra turned to see her back in the long mirror hanging on her closet door. Her years of running, and hoping, even she'd stopped doing either not long ago, did seem to have resulted in-

A butt! Kendra thought, *You kinda have to squint and look at it from the right angle, but a butt!* She set off downstairs in search of waffles, singing "But a butt a but a butt a but a butt…", like a small steam engine working its way up a hill. For the first time ever, she didn't feel like a stretched out version of her younger self.

A once unfamiliar sight was on display in the kitchen - Kendra's mother preparing breakfast. Ever since making captain of her station, she'd had the steady schedule to dabble in something which felt novel for her - domesticity. Her mother put chocolate chips in the batter and a smile on Kendra's face. It lingered as she admired fresh streaks of grey in the Washington matriarch's hair.

It'd be cooler if Mom just had one, long streak, Kendra thought, *But I guess it's okay this way, less a badass, more an actual person.* Kendra's smile evened out when her mother, turning to acknowledge her daughter, worked hard to hide a wince. Six months ago, while she'd been looking for survivors inside a burning school's basement, a manufacturing flaw had allowed a gap in her mother's safety equipment to form at the worst possible time. Boiling hot steam from a burst water pipe had streamed through the opening, searing the left side of her neck.

The kettle sang its usual song and Kendra, sliding on socked feet, went to answer the call. Moving it from the stove to sit upon a nearby oven mitt, she relaxed. Kendra had made a point of handling the kettle whenever she could, unable to fight an irrational fear that, should she let her mother use the device, its much more humble steam might transmute beloved parent particles into long-pig pork cracklings.

"Here you go Dad." She brought him his tea, "Not working today?"

"What gave it away?" Her father gestured to his t-shirt with three wolves howling at the moon, "My uniform?"

"Dad, I love you, but I'm not gonna do the pop cultural archeology necessary to get all your references and stuff."

"Pssh, it's all online." He turned to his wife, who was starting to pry waffles out of the press, "What color was our daughter's hair yesterday? I can't keep track."

"You'd think the giant orange ring in the tub she still hasn't scrubbed out might be your first clue." She answered, filling plates, "Oh and Kendra, I'd like to see that gone before you leave the house today."

"Guild night or date night?" she asked her parents. Sometimes they'd each say a different one and it'd provide a great distraction from anything they'd asked her to do. Not today, alas.

"Guild night," her father answered, "Date night is Saturday."

"Geez, she dyed her eyebrows too." Breakfast was served.

"How?" her father asked, "Trust me, you don't want those chemicals in your eyes."

"Oh I painted it on with a little angle brush, it's a lot better than the scoop thing that comes with the kit." Kendra answered between bites of waffle.

"You've always been such a problem solver, Kendra." Her mother said, "It's made us very proud."

"Yeah." Her father put on a voice she didn't recognize, "Yer a problem solver, Harry!"

Kendra looked at him with mock concern as she continued to shovel chocolate chips, syrup, and waffle into her mouth.

"Seriously?" He said, "You don't get that one?"

"And I've never seen the original Star Wars films! Okay byeeee." Kendra gobbled the last piece of waffle on her plate and fled toward the front door, stepping over the living floor of Dachshunds who rushed to try and join her.

"Kendra, the tub!" Her mother called after her.

"Later!" Kendra called back, "I got a dentist appointment."

The door slammed. Her mother turned to her father.

"I didn't make her an appointment, did you?"

"Nope." Kendra replied, laying back in the dentist's chair, "I want to get rid of this retainer right now, please."

Dr. Juanita Snelgrove asked her if she was sure, again, and repeated in greater detail why it was in her best interest to wear the permanent retainer for another two years. Kendra pouted at the thought.

"I don't think I can stand two more years of…" mouth open, tonguing the wire one last time, she made a swirling gesture around her face, "…this."

In a small park somewhere between the dentist's office and her house, Kendra sat underneath a tree, taking a break from studying A Mind of Its Own by David M. Friedman, running her tongue around the reclaimed real estate inside of her mouth. Val was cross-legged to her left, examining and re-examining a dress, trying to figure out how to attach a lining. Kendra didn't recognize the boy their age sitting under a tree maybe twenty feet across from them. Hair buzzed down like he was in the army, with posture to match, clashed with his loose fitting, plaid skate shorts and white t-shirt. He kept stealing looks which weren't as subtle as he thought they were; she couldn't tell at who; annoyed, she had to know.

Still licking her teeth, Kendra looked over at her friend's dilemma. "Hey, I know you know more about this stuff, but what if you-"

"I got it."

"I just-"

"Wait," Val interrupted, "I thought you were trying not to start sentences with 'I just' anymore?"

The guy looked up again at…Val? *God, he's probably staring at her tits,* Kendra thought, *She should be allowed to show some skin on a hot day without getting creeped on.*

"Yeah, those articles about how to speak with more confidence slid so quickly into policing how women talk." Kendra replied, "I'm gonna keep some of the more assertive phrases, but when it comes to vocal fry etcetera I've decided I'd rather tell men they can damn well listen better."

"Hey I'm a feminist too, just, like," Val spoke quickly, hurrying the words out before any second thoughts could block them off, "you think if you weren't always so aggressive with guys, and I mean that in a couple of ways, you might not drive them off so much?"

"What? Seriously?" Kendra spluttered, "I'm…like I should laugh at bad jokes and…I mean, are you serious?"

The guy took another look at…her? Kendra's brain force-fed her an emotional Neapolitan of irritation at being objectified, pleasure at being the one to get a boy's attention for a change, and worry she'd looked stupid licking her teeth earlier. All this was mixed in the same steaming cauldron of shock as her best friend's unexpected commentary.

"Well, no," Val continued, "but have you considered changing anything else about how you go after guys? You know the definition of insanity…"

"Look, I'm trying!" Kendra replied, "Besides, the thing is to find a guy who likes what you for who you are, though? Right? I just can't find that guy, and also be attracted to him, apparently. I dunno, I dunno."

"Guh, sorry." Val leaned in and whispered, "Forget what I said. I had some serious PS right before I came here."

"Wait, PMS or PS?"

“Period shits.”

In the corner of her eyes Kendra saw the guy steal another glance, she wasn’t sure at who. The idea of skate shorts checking either of them out while they discussed such sexy subject matter broke the mood.

“Ohhhhhh ho ho.” Kendra put her arms around Val’s shoulders, “Ho ho hohhhhh noooo.”

“Bloo hoo hoo.” Val rubbed imaginary tears from her eyes.

Now they were hugging it was even more difficult to tell who the guy was looking at. Val’s phone vibrated. Her mother’s friend was letting her know she could come in to start her apprenticeship right then, if she wanted. Kendra protested, they’d been at the park barely an hour. Val said she should go, reminding Kendra they’d see each other on Saturday, and apologized for being terse with her.

“No problem.” Kendra waved goodbye as Val began to walk away, “Good luck with the dress!”

As soon as Val took a few paces, Skate Shorts lost all interest and barely hung around before getting up to leave. Kendra pulled a fist full of grass out of the earth and tossed it in the air, confetti for her parade of conflicting feelings. Objectification wasn’t cool, being desired was. Well, desire from a welcome source. Kendra also would have liked half the attention she got. Then again, Val had had to deal with so many more losers who thought her figure meant she was promiscuous, not like there’d be anything wrong if she was, and that she wanted to be promiscuous with them. Kendra wanted her friend to finally have a boyfriend and get laid; she didn’t want her friend to leave her behind on the cold island of virginity. Not that being a virgin meant you were Less Than it's just-

"Ugh." Kendra shook her head, wondering if it would clear her thoughts. It just made her dizzy.

Val had been the only one to reply to a torrent of texts sent while sitting in the dentist's waiting room. After making sure Skate Shorts wasn't following her friend, Kendra pulled out her phone. A quick check revealed a mix of non-replies and dismal excuses for not being able to hang out.

Guess it's time to scrub the bathtub, Kendra thought, *if I don't wanna get in bathtrub.*

Seventy Thousand Was Not Enough

Hours later, Kendra lay in bed with her tablet, grateful for the reinforced material in the jumpsuit's knees. Tired from cleaning and weighed down with a stomach full of too much spaghetti, she was trying to prepare for her first year college courses by reading about some of the core concepts her syllabus mentioned. Head resting on a pillow, facing the wall by her bed, she scanned an article explaining the basics of a principle known as co-design. Best she could tell, co-design was a way of resolving dilemmas - usually involving violence - which local communities weren't able to solve and outside parties lacked the knowledge or commitment to properly understand. Instead, both locals and outsiders acknowledged neither of them had all the answers and worked together while playing to their respective strengths. Letting the book close on an index finger, Kendra wondered if co-design could be applied to individuals instead of, say, a coastal village with a large drug problem and a well-meaning but clueless NGO. What if she and a boy virgin could just calmly, rationally discuss the issue? Then maybe-

Remembering what Paul said in her hotel room two years ago, Kendra closed the book.

"Kendra!" Her mother called, "Your favorite movie is on! Come here!"

Kendra snorted a quick laugh, "Sure!"

Kendra knew her mom could barely recall not being able to just watch what she wanted, when she wanted to. What she had were fond memories of Kendra's grandparents calling her, as a little girl, out of her room whenever something they wanted to share with her, or knew she liked, came on. It was an excuse to spend more time with their daughter and, a generation down, it was an even more obvious excuse when Kendra's mother must have simply selected what was bound to be Annie Hall from one of the half dozen streaming services they subscribed to. Kendra didn't mind, though. It was just a less direct way of saying "I love you and want to spend time with you."

Kendra came in to the living room just after her mother must have hit play, trying to add to the illusion of the film being on owing to coincidence. Sure enough, there was 1970's Woody Allen standing in front of a beige wall and telling them his relationship with Annie had recently ended. Kendra now knew what a scuzzbag he'd been in real life, and refused to watch any of his other works, however she didn't want to let this taint her enjoyment of a film she'd been watching with her mother for just over half her years on this Earth.

"Hey, Mom," Kendra gestured to let the film keep playing while she spoke, "Why didn't you and Dad ever have 'The Talk' with me?"

"You were so inquisitive and set on working things out for yourself, we figured there was no need unless you asked us. You never did." Her mother kept her eyes on the screen, "Why? Do you want to ask me something?"

Kendra said "No." so quickly, she silently cursed herself for closing a door she assumed she couldn't open again.

"Did you talk with Greg?"

"Yes. Mostly about consent and how manhood wasn't something he had to prove to anyone, or even participate in if he didn't see himself that way."

After Annie Hall ended, her mother put on some nineties sitcom which had been in syndication longer than Kendra had been alive; a show where a group of emotionally constipated twenty-somethings hung around the same few places all the time, including apartments none of them could possibly afford. She couldn't stand it, and the episode her mother chose was beyond intolerable. First the friends were embarrassing someone by looking at a photo album of their baby pictures, which Kendra couldn't even begin to relate to since the baby pictures of her and everyone else she knew had been put online by their parents, in real time, for anyone to see. Then some sub-plot, about two of the friends being adorable and kissing a lot, kicked in and Kendra shot up to go to the kitchen. Standing by the fridge she realized she had nothing to do in there, just having wanted to be away from the sight of photogenic people making each other feel good about themselves.

"Oh, stop being embarrassed!" Her mother called after her, "It's just kissing, Jesus."

"They're kissing Jesus?" Kendra called back, staying in the kitchen.

"Don't be a smart-ass, you know what I-" Kendra's mother, and her daughter, heard Kendra's Dad's swearing waft up from the part of the basement where they'd moved the family computer, "Kendra, why don't you go online and help your father?"

"Will do!"

Swooping up the stairs and back into her bedroom, Kendra happily logged on to help her father with a raid. Usually people in his guild were being terrible about coordinating their attacks against the end of raid boss, so Kendra would slide in and help lead by example. Once on the server, she used a scroll of teleportation to get her Ork Shaman, Special K, to her Dad's location deep in a Necromancer's tomb-dungeon. Arriving with all her buffs already activated she looked around for some giant demon or whatever. She found the guild; the battle was already over and they were all gathered in a circle around two members facing each other; a soviet-themed steampunk cyborg ork and a bruiser of an elf, carrying a sword taller than she was. The cyborg ork was standing back up, as if he'd been crouching, and the elf was still - presumably while the user was typing the command for a gesture of her own.

She really should have a few hot-keyed gestures so she can communicate quicker in combat. Kendra thought, *Sheesh.*

The elf nodded enthusiastically. The ork jumped up very high and then skittered around a bit on the spot. His player must have been too excited to handle his keyboard properly. Some of this excitement spread into the rest of the guild, who erupted in a display of enthusiastic congratulations both across the guild's private chat and their character's gestures.

Kendra opened a private chat window with her father. “Dad, why were you swearing?”

“It was happy swearing, I couldn’t believe Leningrad Cowboy was actually proposing to Baby Lulu…and she said yes! Can’t believe it. They met right here in the guild and, lucky them, both live in the same city.”

“What,” Kendra replied in the chat, then finished out loud, “the fuck.”

“Hey have you ever talked to any boys on here? ‘Cause net safety is a real-”

Kendra quit out of the game entirely, left her tablet plugged into the speakers on her desk, then walked over to the bean bag chair she’d set up in the corner of her room whose walls she’d covered with milk crate bookshelves.

“Woof.” she said, throwing herself at the bean bag like it had done something wrong. Just before logging out, she’d glanced at the guild chat window and saw someone saying how the ‘diamond ring’ for the proposal had been a super rare diamond sword item Leningrad had bought from a South Korean item farmer for almost a thousand dollars. Real, goddamn dollars.

“Christ.” Kendra said, blinking hard, trying to re-set, and reached up behind her head to fumble around for a book her father recommended. Five minutes later and she decided Fight Club, by Chuck Palahniuk, wasn’t her thing. The whole big reveal just pissed her off with how much it was supposed to blow her mind, instead of actually doing so. She felt bad, it hadn’t been long since she’d also had to give up on a door wedge of Hunter S. Thompson he’d put under her nose. She’d always be grateful for her dad making sure she got into reading in the first place, even if she couldn't always love what he loved, and sometimes wished there was a way to please others by being or doing what they wanted without compromising herself.

Not sure which book in her to-read pile to start next, Kendra sunk down, sighed, and pulled out her phone. Camilla had forwarded her a video, so she tilted her favorite rectangle sideways and clicked through. It was filmed late at night by someone in the passenger seat of a white sedan cruising along a Florida highway. At first it was some kind of "Hi Mom!" vacation check-in, then the driver yelled at them to look back through the rear window. A blur as the camera spun around along with its owner, some frantic pinch-pull zooming was done, then the reason Camilla linked Kendra to the video came roaring into view. Five guys driving a large pick-up truck had placed a winch in the back, running several lengths of heavy gauge chain to wrap around a thirty foot tall fiberglass restaurant mascot for a local chain Kendra didn't recognize. Thanks to them, a giant anthropomorphic chicken waitress, proudly holding up a plate filled with the wings of its brethren, was skidding along the highway at ninety miles an hour. As the truck raced to maintain the momentum preventing the chicken waitress from tipping forward to crush them, it swung up beside the sedan, just one lane between them. Pausing the video, Kendra was able to read the large, red bubble letters on the giant chicken's apron - DIRTY BIRD WYNGS AND THYNGS.

The next moment giant chicken feet swung perilously close to the sedan, freaking out the driver, and sent them skidding off the highway to fishtail along the dirt. Kendra couldn't help being impressed by how steady the passenger held her phone while she screamed and the car juddered to a halt. One last glimpse of the giant chicken being pulled off into the distance and the video ended, a thumbnail for an actual Dirty Bird Wyngs and Thyngs commercial overlaying itself as a recommendation to watch next.

Jesus, Kendra thought, *that's a real adventure. Not sneaking joints and beer in the woods or whatever. How do I find that kind of thing around here?*

A sigh and a habitual thumb stroke later found Kendra watching Corey Newkirk, one of her regular stable of video game longplay boys. Listening to them talk and joke their way through games was a pleasure and their occasional vlogs or sketches were a nice excuse to enjoy looking at them. Their hair, poofy or gelled, their pore-less skin, almost always white for some reason, and the actual physical remove made them less intimidating than the Will Daniels of the world and less gross than the Pauls.

Today, though, she realized she'd extracted the last of the sugar rushes her crushes on Corey and his kind could give her. The distance was alienating now, not comforting. Mostly, watching Corey make one bad choice after another in the construction of a fortress designed to repel zombies, the video just made her want to reach through the screen and play the game herself.

"Hmmmm." Kendra hmmmmd.

Away from videos and over to one of the social media sites not yet invaded by a wave of parents and grandparents, she went to her own profile at first. Satisfied by the amount of attention a picture of her new hair color had received, and dissatisfied by the lack of qualitatively measurable attention for her sharing of an article about Guineau-Bisseau's booming drug trade, Kendra read some of the latest news on her main feed. It seemed Camilla and the girl she'd taken to prom, Lauren, were having a very public, very passive-aggressive disagreement as to how faithful Camilla had been in the weeks since they'd surprised everyone by beating out several popular couples, all in much more established relationships, to be voted Prom Queens.

The girls were being an unsubtle kind of subtle in their posts. With Lauren wondering what makes "some people" feel the need to look at others when they already have a perfectly wonderful partner, and Camilla commenting on how wedding dresses and straight jackets are both the same color, it wasn't hard for those who knew them to get what they were referring to. It all seemed crazy to Kendra.

It's been almost two months since prom and Lauren still has their prom queen photo as her profile picture, Kendra thought, *Plus there's dumbass Owen managing to look good while photo-bombing the thing.*

Staring at Owen, and the grin he gave while popping up in the space between Camilla and Lauren's crowns of spray-painted cardboard, Kendra said "Nnnno, no, no, no thank you, no."

She than began to thumb out a post about how unfair it was that boys have all the power because they become less emotionally invested in girls than they do in them, deciding Paul didn't count because of his grossness, only to delete it two seconds after sharing. Leaving her phone to have the bean bag chair all to itself, Kendra walked over to her desk and woke up her tablet. Fifteen minutes later she'd copied four of Owen's handsomest head shots from photos he'd been tagged in and stuck them over the faces of four nude men going to town on each other in a hot tub. Kendra couldn't decide if she found it arousing, funny, or both.

"Farousing," Kendra said, "Arfunny?"

She had a long moment of staring and thinking about creating an anonymous account to share the picture online. Deciding it might come across as homophobic, Kendra deleted everything she'd done.

"Hornlarious?" She said, carrying the tablet to her bed, "Oh, who cares?"

Once more Kendra lay on her side, facing the wall, and placed her head in the groove she'd left in her pillow. Frustrated by settling into the same position as earlier, she grunted while pushing herself around to face the rest of her room, head at the opposite end of the bed; a bed Kendra had never shared with anyone except Salvador Doggy, Honey Garlic, and Spicy Italian.

She hadn't slept with a boy there or anywhere else, not when she was thirteen, like Gwen, nor sixteen "like normal," or seventeen, or at prom or any other point in her high school career. She couldn't stand the thought of having to move her personal goal posts any further than where they currently sat, just after the end of summer party she'd be attending on the coming Saturday. All four years of high school, with no real dates, no relationships, not even that casual sex thing anyone would think came free in the mail the way so many people carried on. Imagining sitting alone, denied all human contact in a featureless, moonlit cube of a room, Kendra felt like she was seeing her future.

"Oh for the love of farts, can I think about anything else at all, pleaaaaase?" She said to her tablet.

Kendra logged into her account at infohose.com and began browsing her favorite forums and sub-hoses. Despite herself, she moved past discussion of the upcoming Dance Panic 2001 game, and went straight to seek sweet, sweet affirmation over in the role-playing game forums. Internet Stranger Compliment Dopamine was triggered by a comment underneath a fantasy adventure she'd recently written and uploaded for other game-master's to run. A "Sacha" said they'd downloaded the adventure and were going to spend time making some elaborate props before running for their friends. Kendra replied, letting them know she hoped it would go well, then looked at Sacha's profile to see where they were posting from.

Greenville.

Even though it could be any number of Greenville's other than the one Azealia moved to, this still reminded her of things Kendra was trying to distract herself from. With the RPG forums temporarily tainted, she moved on to her most well trod corner of infohose.com; Weird Sex Stuff. Never one to pass up a chance to be annoyed by members of the real life anti-sex league, she chose to follow a link someone had posted to an article about preparations being made for the Olympics being held in Baghdad in two years time.

The usual crowd of conservative religious folk were pressuring the government into taking special measures to prevent fraternizing between athletes in the Olympic Village currently being constructed. Kendra didn't understand why athletes sleeping with each other was of any more concern to these types than anybody else daring to enjoy their time on Earth. Then Kendra's mouth slowly fell open as she read on.

Having no social life thanks to obsessive training for four, or more, years made people lonely, apparently. Competing in front of the world, trying to break records set by the best of humanity, was a massive rush that made most athletes seek pre-competition stress release and/or a post-competition come down, apparently. Lots of excess energy to burn off in an environment where they finally get some privacy from trainers and reporters, apparently. At the 2000 Sydney Games, the usual order of condoms for the Olympic Village had had to be raised another thirty-thousand because seventy-thousand condoms just hadn't been enough, apparently. One charming athlete said even if someone's face was just a seven, their body was off the chart, apparently. Due to the different requirements of all the various sports, there was a huge variety of these off the chart bodies, apparently.

Win a gold medal and sleep with all sorts of Greek gods, and every other nationality, why not?

There were a few pictures of the most photogenic athletes. Kendra's mother had done a decent job of teaching her daughter to treat the appearances of movie stars and models as having as much to do with real life as the U.S.S. Enterprise or a horde of dragons soaring through the sky. She hadn't said anything about upwards of ten thousand professional athletes with bodies that not only looked incredible, they could do incredible things. Oh sure, they might fall in love and have the strictness of training make them unable to see each other for another four years, but Kendra felt this would be a pretty nice problem to have.

"Why the hell did I give up running?" She whispered harshly, hearing her parents chattering in the bathroom as they prepared for bed. Kendra didn't really think she could have competed at anything approaching the Olympic level. This didn't stop her from wondering if maybe, at a much younger age, she'd known what the article told her was an open secret then perhaps…

I would have had the right motivation, she thought.

Reading stories like this, stories she'd usually embarrass herself by repeating to some boy, used to be a vent for her frustrations or a way of living vicariously. Now it was like seeing cute couples in the park or on TV. Reading about this mobile, temporary, bi-annual sex Valhalla burned brighter and hotter than seeing a thousand shows or films featuring the world of sophisticated, inner-city sex lives going on far and away from her, far and away from anything she could even imagine.

Kendra put the tablet to sleep and slid it onto the floor. She tried to feel a ghost of the sensation of kissing William Daniels. Desperate, she even tried to remember what it had felt like when Paul had touched her. She ran a finger along her lower lip. Nothing. All the expiry dates on the memories in her paltry pantry of physical contact had been passed.

Looking across to the other side of the room, her eyes were

drawn to a glow-in-the dark figurine on the floor. It was a three inch tall green man with a superhero's build and a crest of white hair, something a much younger Kendra had seen fit to hide in the secret compartment of the play-structure at Woodenmeyer Bi-Centennial. He must have been something she'd saved from long before grade eight, a companion from the days when sex was just some weird hugging thing adults did and it took up less mental real-estate than her curiosity about how bees flew or if something as long as a summer month could possibly ever end.

Now the ecosystem of her mind felt smothered beneath the urban sprawl of her needs.

Kendra closed her eyes, harder, screwed up her face, let out a small gasp, breathed in, then out. Opening them she searched for a flickering, yellow lizard she remembered seeing slowly stepping through the darkness in the shadows of her room. A dimly recalled parade of androgynous red humanoids came to mind, but didn't appear on the floor by the bookshelves. There was just the glow-in-the-dark, green plastic man, his figure a parody of what she'd been taught to desire.

Kendra rubbed her eyes, seeing dark red spirals twist through blackness.

And looked. Just the green man.

Kendra rubbed her eyes again, the knuckles of her index fingers becoming wet.

And looked. Just the green man.

Kendra rubbed her eyes again.

Harder.

Constellations

Kendra felt a wet, wide flap of green flesh slap across her eye and a long, pencil-thin finger whip across her thigh.

"Oh, man!" Kendra stopped to twist the thin branch off of the tree, bending it back and forth until it snapped off, and tossed it deeper into the woods. Val, seeing Camilla move in to help, fought her urge to do the same, and stayed up ahead with Celine.

"You tell that tree who's boss, Kendra." Camilla watched as Kendra swiped at the higher branch, with its moist leaves.

"Guh, it was gonna rip my tights and, hey," She turned to face Camilla, "can you see if it smeared the blue on my eye-brow?"

"Looks fine."

"Good, shit's expensive. Makeup, leggings, birth control, tampons, nice underwear, and, may I say it again - *make-up*. Feminine performance isn't a game for the broke!" Kendra complained, hugging herself, "I'm seriously reconsidering my stance on splitting the bill. Maybe boys *should* always pay for the date."

Celine stopped, then walked back with Val keeping one step behind her. Despite several strong suggestions from the others, the youngest of the group was once again wearing her rabbit onesie. Kendra wondered if Celine hoped some of the woodland creatures would think her one of their own, and feel safe enough to come close for a petting.

"Are you okay, Kendra?" Celine asked.

"Yeah." Kendra shivered, "I'm just not sure about this outfit."

An hour earlier, rain beating on the bathroom mirror, Val had been blowing purple-flavored bubbles while watching Kendra assemble her armor for the evening. She'd earned a few minutes rest, having just spent what felt like a year twisting Kendra's blue and white locks into a Swiss braid. Next were blue eyebrows, followed by clear contact lenses, then ocean blue and gold glitter giving Kendra a variation on freckles she'd fantasized about having since reading Pippy Longstocking. She felt they went nicely with the constellations decorating her nails. A hop and a skip down from plain lip gloss, the tall collar of her burgundy dress shirt poked up from within a white suede sport coat she'd spent all but the last thirty dollars of her August spending money on.

Val had altered it to flatter her friend's figure, then set to reviving an old pair of Kendra's white jeans as cut-offs. These were held up by a black belt with the "Everything Is Bigger in Texas" buckle Kendra refused to remove; her finding the idea of bragging about a cavernous vagina too funny to listen to Valory's pleas.

Trusty gold tights covered the rest of her legs, leading down to take root in a pair of thick white sneakers Kendra couldn't believe had made her nostalgic enough to buy them. The ghosts of Heather Grey air-show, art gallery, and museum sweaters had floated around her head as she'd approached the cashier.

Five minutes after her parents left for their date night, Kendra turned to her friend and said "Okay, now to step up my game."

She removed the dress shirt and grabbed the cotton candy blue body paint which had been used on her eyebrows. With some assistance from Val, and a reference picture on her phone, Kendra drew three lines across the top of either side of her chest. The top and bottom lines were narrow, while the middle line was about three inches thick, and all of them came to a single point. Curved along the top like an airplane wing and starting at just beneath her armpits, they ended so as to leave a one inch wide valley of clear skin running down her sternum.

"Once this dries, the jacket goes back on and we can leave." Kendra leaned against the bathroom counter, "Now you know why I wanted the jacket to fit so tightly. I don't want to give more of a show than I want to give, you know?"

"Jesus," Val stood back, taking her friend in, "I can't tell if you look like something out of European fashion magazines, or anime."

Kendra smiled.

Kendra frowned, "It's cold."

"It's hot." Camilla countered, patting her friend on the back.

"Well," Kendra huffed, "it's not like I could put anymore lipstick on this pig."

"Oh, cut it out." Val said, "Besides, we could have put some gold glitter down the middle."

"Right?" Kendra agreed, "Damn, that would've been good.

But maybe too much?"

Kendra looked around for something, anything else to talk about. As luck would have it, they were a few feet from a very familiar disturbance in the dirt. Asking Camilla if her and Owen still kept a cooler buried near the school, she learned the secret had gotten out. It kept getting raided so they had to stop. Celine said her entire homeroom that year had known about the cooler in the woods.

"Hey Val, we waiting for Nat?" Camilla asked.

"Uh…yeah, I mean, we don't have to but, uh, I guess that's technically what we're doing by standing here." Val looked away, "I dunno, I'm not her keeper."

"I hate having to go anywhere near school in the summer." Celine complained.

"So make the city open a new bus line closer to Talib's house." Nat said, emerging from the shadows with both hands tucked into her hoodie. Having refused to rush, she was just now catching up to the group. Plodding along, the usual twist of smoke tumbling up from her mouth to the moon, Val's sister pulled up the brim on her baseball cap and saw Kendra's outfit.

"Damn, Ken, you want the boys to stare at you, huh?"

"Haha yeah," Camilla gave Nat a quick squeeze on the shoulder, "Kendra's real thirsty."

"Shut up." Kendra pulled her jacket closed and tried to walk away at a casual pace, only more-so.

The Party

Talib was the kind of guy who everyone knew and few people were close to. Kendra hadn't quite believed the invite she received was sincere, had assumed he'd just hit "Select All" on his friend list, which included half the damn school, and let'er rip. Some quick messaging confirmed he had, actually, very much meant to invite her. Even nine weeks after graduation, Kendra still hadn't gotten used to the unexpected notoriety she'd gained in her last year of high school. Exasperation had been confused with confidence, earning a respect for how her tongue and her wardrobe had become sharper, each saying things even the popular kids didn't feel sure enough to say.

The front lawn of Talib's mother's townhouse had a scattering of party goers doing a bad job hiding their beers and being subtle about passing around a cigar. Kendra and her squad were given a few glances as they crossed to the front door; nobody waved or said hello. The first floor of Talib's house was deceptively small looking, with most of its floorspace consumed by a laundry and storage room. Other than the stairs to their right, there was a small TV room. Talib popped out of this, having just put an almost terminal look of disinterest on a drama club girl Kendra didn't know the name of. Eager to escape an awkward moment, his skinny frame jostled around within a gigantic rugby shirt and tiny pair of black shorts as he fought to navigate the infestation of sneakers covering the modest common area. Running fingers through close cropped curls, he smiled in his way that made anyone want to listen to him - for a while, at least.

He greeted the girls. Camilla gave him a high five, then introduced Val, Nat, and Celine. Loving her outfit, Talib tweaked one of Celine's rabbit ears, she pretended not to mind, then he offered to give them a tour of the house.

"Sure!" Kendra said, searching to see where his eyes settled on her. She wished she was better at following the eye-lines of boys.

Up and around a narrow rectangle of stairs, they came to the second, main floor of the house. Right of the stairs was a communal closet which hadn't an inch to spare for any more fall coats or sneaker kudzu. Talib pointed past this, toward the kitchen which took up almost half of the floor. There his mother was finishing baking several trays of fresh, chocolate chip cookies to go with the oatmeal raisin ones she'd already stacked high on the kitchen table. She gave everyone a big smile, then turned back to the cookies.

The other half of the main floor was a large living area which exited onto a modest balcony. A TV sat at the opposite end, bookshelves lining the far wall. The balcony itself had a most interesting, temporary feature - a keg.

"Nice." Kendra nodded in the direction of the balcony.

"Whoah, your mom's okay with you having that?" Celine asked.

"Yeah, she's pretty cool." Talib replied.

"She knows he'd be doing it SOMEwhere, so she'd rather he barf himself stupid in the safety of his own home." Camilla added, getting a playful punch in the shoulder, "Lil' Talib's mommy wuvs him very much."

Nat split off and went straight to the kitchen while Talib led the rest of them up another flight of narrow stairs. On the top floor there was a narrow hallway which led like a landing strip to Talib's bedroom. On the right hand side was a bathroom already sporting a decent line-up. On the left hand there was a spare closet, then Talib's sister's bedroom, and just before Talib's room was the door to where his mother slept.

Kendra and the others who hadn't visited before were all delighted by how Talib's mother had covered every inch of the walls, and most of the doors, with large, glossy, inspirational posters. Cats told them to hang in there. Captain Picard told them if they had a dream, it was up to them to "make it so". Space itself told them to shoot for the moon, because even if the girls missed then they'd land among the stars. It was kind of perfect.

"Having your mom's room beside yours can't be helpful with ladies." Kendra said.

"Naw, love always finds a way." Talib chuckled, "So yeah, that's the house! You guys want some beer?"

Camilla was already going down the stairs. The rest followed her back to the main floor. Celine split off to fill her felt paws with cookies, joining Nat, Tim and Richard by the table. Kendra glanced at Richard, then caught a glimpse of turquoise hair on the other side of the dividing wall; Owen was over by the keg. Seeing her friend, Camilla headed toward him, pulling Kendra and Val along with her.

Taking in the crowd around her, Kendra saw at least eight members of the rugby team, three more girls from the drama club, Kevin, Mary, and another half dozen she didn't know. Eventually she had to look at Owen; it would have been strange not to, now she was standing in front of him. By her side Camilla, whose hand jerked as Val removed herself from the Goth's tight, lace-covered grip. Otherwise it was mostly guys by the keg; a lot of them were men-in-progress; not Owen.

How the hell did he get so fit? Kendra wondered, *Where's the schlubby giant who punched out the crazy homeless guy?*

He was still there, of course, but had revealed piercing eyes by combing his now turquoise hair up into a pompadour, then shaving the sides. Owen's carefully cropped beard matched the color of his hair. Kendra tried to hate him for wearing the same Goodwill tuxedo he'd worn to prom, finding out she couldn't. Coming out from under the legs of black dress pants in desperate need of an ironing, she saw a very large pair of white, high-backed Keds with black laces bearing a pattern of swirling cartoon ghosts. Camilla reached up to tighten the bow-tie around his neck.

"Hey jerk-off," She said, "get up to any good jerkin' off lately?"

"Oh, you know," He replied, "nothing to write home about."

"I'd like to read those letters," Kendra said, "those letters you write to your parents about the real good soft-serve, self-serve handies." Everyone laughed as Kendra went on to describe how Owen's handwriting suffered since, she presumed, he wrote these letters while continuing to play with himself. When the laughter paused, they took turns crawling around each other to get at the keg through the balcony's sliding glass door. Soon everyone had a red plastic cup in their hand, filled with something Talib, as he passed by to get some cookies, bragged was from a Canadian brewery in Hamilton.

Val decided to ask something she knew was important to Kendra when it became plain her pal wasn't going to, despite her having brought up concern over his presence roughly two hundred times while Val had been braiding her hair earlier, "So Owen, is Will Daniels coming by tonight?"

"Nnnnnno." Owen took a deep pull from his cup, "I think he's at another party or something."

"Ohhh." Camilla rubbed his hair, "Such loyalty!"

"What?" Kendra said, already finishing her drink and squeezing by for another.

"Idiot left in his car for Greenville last night." Camila explained, "He's probably there by now, making one last big gesture to try and keep his relationship with Azealia alive."

Kendra slouched against the sliding door, let out a small sigh of relief, and started her second beer.

"Jesus Camilla," Owen said, "I thought you two were friends?"

"We are! We talk at least once a week." She protested, "And good friends don't keep secrets from each other, fight over potential partners, or leave bullshit un-called upon."

Val listened closely. "Uh, Camilla, what bullshit are you calling Azealia on? Or Will?"

"Well Valory," Camilla beamed, "I'm calling them both on the bullshit of trying to keep a long-distance relationship going for just over two years of their all too short time as teenagers. It's obviously not gonna work out, and now isn't the time to basically marry each other."

"Yyyyyeah, I think Azealia was looking at teaching English in China or South Korea or something. If so, she'd be leaving pretty soon." Owen added, "Will is my main guy and Azzy's great. It's just hard to see him chase her so damn hard."

Owen tapped Camilla on the shoulder and gestured toward the other end of the room, by the TV. Two of the Gothic Lolita girls - whose names Kendra could never be bothered to learn - had appeared, somehow with and not with Camilla's prom date, Lauren. All three waved. Kendra thought she heard Owen whisper "Come on." to Camilla before putting his arm across her back and heading across.

"We're gonna say hi." Owen said over his shoulder, "Talk to you later?"

"Sure, why not?" Kendra replied.

"You good?" Val asked.

"Yeah." Kendra finished her second beer, went straight to pouring a third, "How 'bout you? You've been kinda quiet, spacey, fidgety-"

"-sneezy, sleepy, dopey, bashful, grumpy, happy…doc." Val interrupted, "I'm just distracted by how soon so many of us are gonna leave town or whatever, I guess."

"It is pretty messed up." Kendra said, "I hear cookies solve all your problems?"

As they moved to the kitchen table, Kendra gave a little wave to Richard. He gave an unenthusiastic wave back and walked away, taking a path that made it look like there was an impenetrable, invisible field centered around Valory. Tim gave a conciliatory shrug, then followed. If Valory knew what this was all about, Kendra couldn't read it in her face.

Everyone at the table cheered, thanking Talib's mother for the cookies as she smiled, bowed, and left to spend the rest of the evening at a next door neighbor's where - Talib informed them - she was likely to fall asleep while drinking wine and binge-watching musicals with two of her girlfriends.

Talib turned back to two of the other drama girls he was trying to impress. Celine grabbed a pair of small plates for Val and Kendra, almost dropping both with her onesie's smooth paws. Small-talk among the girls died down when they saw who was heading their way.

"Oh, hey Gwen." Celine said.

"Hey girls!" Gwen strutted over, making a show of picking up a single oatmeal and raisin cookie, "You know I was just saying to someone before I came by, isn't it such a pain when a guy cums before you do, then he falls asleep? I mean, don't you just hate it when that happens?"

God Dammit, she knows none of us have had sex, Kendra thought, *swallowing a mouthful of cookie harder than was comfortable, I'm trying to practice Shine Theory and all, but…*

Seeing Celine blushing and Val trying to find something to

look at in the distance, Kendra washed her mouth out with beer, then pounced.

"Hey Gwen, don't you just hate it when nobody likes you? Like, nobody at all?" Kendra spoke firmly and loudly, making sure Talib and the drama girls would turn to pay attention, "Must be pretty rough to think about, when you're not having orgasms, huh?"

"Well," Gwen replied, "Kevin likes me."

Kendra sputtered. She hadn't thought much of Kevin for a long time, but it still burned her metaphorical bunions. Not sure what to say, she was grateful when one of the drama girls - Sidney? - tapped in.

"Because you MADE him like you, you fuckin' bitch!" Sidney yelled, much, much louder than Kendra had just been. Wary of the party being brought down by melodrama, Talib stepped in.

"Hey, whoah, girls! Tonight's about having a good time." He guided them both to the balcony, "Let me get you some drinks and we'll all just chill, okay?"

The remaining drama girl followed, keen to see what would happen next.

"Wow." Celine said, peeling away to get her first beer and follow the show.

"Man, I have no idea what's going on there." Kendra said, finishing her beer, "Well, obviously I have some idea but you get what I'm saying."

Val took a small sip from her own red cup, "There's always stories going on just outside your peripheral vision, ones other than your own, you know?"

Kendra stared at her friend. "Okay, for real, is there anything you want to-"

A few rugby players, who'd been watching the excitement from the living room, came over to get some cookies. Their laughter and banter smothered Kendra's words. Val made a dismissive gesture, then directed her friend's attention to a new arrival coming up the stairs, down the other end from where they were standing.

"Oh geez, it's Mary." Kendra had curdled on Mary since seeing her spend the past year with an honest-to-God boyfriend, a Chris who insisted on being called Christopher.

"Is her sun-dress made from bedsheets?" Val asked, looking at the faded, cartoon sea creatures and patches on Mary's outfit, "Like, childhood bedsheets?"

Christopher greeted Mary with a long kiss, the fingers of his left hand scrabbling toward her behind like a hungry pet who just heard their food bowl rattle. Mary, putting her arms around him like someone in love, didn't seem to mind. Seeing this, Kendra forget everything she'd ever read about Shine Theory, about women focusing on making each other look good instead of tearing each other down.

"Jesus, childhood bedsheets." Kendra snorted, grabbing an abandoned bottle of beer between the towers of cookies, "What'll Chris-toe-fur think when he gets under there and sees the lingerie made from her old diapers?"

Overhearing her, some of the rugby players laughed. Kendra soaked it up, brewing something sharp and sour when mixing in assumptions of Mary sleeping with Christopher. Mary, having sex, maybe for the whole year! The lanky goon had just crushed on him in science class, then literally crushed him against his locker with a bear hug until they both tittered their way into the beginnings of a relationship. Tall, gawky Mary - who stood two full inches over Christopher - with her weird outbursts and Goodwill clothes. Well, not like Kendra's Goodwill suits, of course, that's not the same thing.

"It was so weird when she gave him a bouquet of sunflowers at prom." Val said, tearing into an oatmeal-raisin.

"Yeah and what a prize she's got there, hiding that stupid butt-chin of his under…," Kendra gesticulated at her target, not caring if he or Mary noticed, "I mean, what's with that goatee? Looks like he scalped someone's nutsack and chewed through the middle."

One of the larger rugby players let out a hearty "Oh! Damn!"

Mary and Christopher turned their heads.

Val looked at Kendra, "Careful, you're getting kinda mean."

Kendra wasn't sure how to reply, losing her chance as Val went off in search of another drink, and the loud rugby player further endorsed her burn with a hearty pat on the back. Kendra stayed and enjoyed entertaining the guys with a few more cutting remarks about their now-former classmates, then slid away when the discussion moved on. Camilla was still talking with her Gothic Lolita buddies, who Kendra knew didn't share Camilla's feelings about Azealia and Will's relationship. The two Lolitas, whose names Kendra now wished she could remember, had given her frosty looks right up through grad.

Celine was passed out on the living room couch. A quick

inspection confirmed a lack of foul play, the big bunny rabbit had just done what she always did when she so much as sniffed a beer or stayed up past ten pm and here she was having done both. Mulling over what to do, Kendra was approached by Tim.

"Hey Kendra, have you seen Richard?"

"No. You seen Val?"

"She just went upstairs."

"Okay." Kendra took Celine's half-empty cup and finished its contents, "Listen, can you keep an eye on Celine? I'm not comfortable leaving her alone, you know?"

"Uh, sure." Tim scratched his forearm, "Why don't you, though?"

"I gotta talk to Val." Kendra replied, "It's important, I think."

"Alright." Tim sat down beside Celine.

"Behave yourself, huh?"

"Geez, Kendra," Tim blanched, "I'm not a rapist or whatever you think Paul is."

"I never said, he was - he just…" Kendra caught herself, rallied, "He expressed his feelings inappropriately and wouldn't listen to what I was saying. We each had…have a very similar problem and we could have been there for each other, as friends. Instead he got angry and revealed the tip of an iceberg of resentment I never even knew existed before!"

Tim and Kendra just stared at each other for a moment. She was proud for articulating herself so well, untangling at least one ball of frustration, smoothing it out into a straightforward breakdown of what had caused it in the first place.

"So you'll forgive me if I have some trust issues." She continued, "Still, I did ask you in the first place, right?"

Tim squinted, then nodded. Kendra patted his shoulder, before heading for the stairwell. On the way up she passed Gwen sitting on her own, being a pain even when quiet and still - an obstacle people had to step over. Once at the top of the stairs, Kendra saw Val slip into the washroom. Owen was waiting to go in next. It wasn't the golden light of dawn spreading across a verdant field of lush, green grass decorated with morning dew, but the hall light still managed to make him look fantastic.

"Ahhhhh." Kendra said under her breath, wondering what his beard would feel like, "Fuck. Me."

"Kendra," Gwen called from the stairwell, "what'd I tell you about sticking to guys on your level?"

"You know, I was feeling kinda sad and angry on my way here." Kendra hissed, "I'm not sad anymore. Thanks."

Squaring her shoulders, chin up, Kendra left Gwen behind and stepped right up.

"Oh, hey Kendra," Owen said, "I meant to say earlier, I really like that body paint tattoo thing you have going on there."

"Been staring at my chest, huh?" She purred.

"Ugh!" Owen put his head back, "Man, I knew you'd say that. Come on, you put the paint right there."

"It's okay, I know."

"And," He looked back down again, careful to stay on her eyes, "I just thought it was cool. Like there are these claws ready to pull your chest open, exposing your heart to the world."

Holy Crap, I was just referencing one of my Dad's old comics. Kendra thought, *If anybody asks, I'll tell'em what Owen said.*

"Aw, wow, Owen," Kendra had to look away, "I don't remember you being so eloquent when we all went downtown together. Remember that?"

"Sure."

Kendra enjoyed just being silent with Owen for a moment. Then an idea sparked as she passed her eyes over the inspirational posters. Standing on her toes and placing her hands on his broad shoulders, she whispered it in Owen's ear. Much to her delight, he laughed so hard he hunched over low enough she could lay her feet flat on the floor again. Her face having been so close to his, she was also pleased to confirm her suspicions of him smelling wonderful. Kendra admitted to herself she'd been crushing on him for at least the past year; having held back for fear of another painful rejection or an unfamiliar, even more unwelcome, experience.

"Yes," He said when he regained his composure, "I'm down. Just gotta go to the washroom first."

"Aw, come on Owen," Kendra let her hands slide down from his shoulders to his firm chest, then raised her voice to make sure Val would hear through the door, "girls take forever in the bathroom!"

A pause. Val played her part, "Yes! That is true. About girls."

"Sure," Owen said, "but I still have to-"

"Hey, no problem." Kendra stepped toward the stairs, trying her best to look like a coy forest nymph, having no idea if she was pulling it off, "Just whip out your male privilege in an alley along the way. I won't mind."

"Ha. Wow. You know Kendra, I've always liked," Owen said,

starting to follow, "how you're always absolutely yourself."

Kendra turned away, so he wouldn't see the gigantic smile he'd put on her face, thinking, *Wow, Owen, you keep saying things like that and I'll keep on having the best night of my life. Deal?*

"See you later Gwen." Kendra said, stepping over her former friend on the way down the stairs, Owen in tow, "We're gonna go out for a bit."

"Sure," Gwen said, glaring, "have fun."

All The Sex

Around the corner of the strip mall at the end of Talib's street, Kendra waited while Owen peed. Staring at the crescent moon, she remembered how her father had once joked about real intimacy being when your partner didn't care about walking in on you in the bathroom. Thinking it over, she decided it was far too soon for her to barge in on Owen as he urinated between two parked mini-vans.

Still, maybe it would show him how comfortable and cool I am if I peed at the same time, She thought, *where he could hear me? Like, in solidarity?*

Owen zipped up and joined her. "Sorry, could you hear?"

Kendra shrugged.

"Gross." Owen put his hands in his pockets, then tilted his head toward the convenience store. Kendra nodded and they went over.

Rushing past the usual junk food, Kendra spotted what they'd come for and burst out laughing.

"I can't believe people still make these things, never mind buying them!"

"I can believe it. You know I had to find a fax machine so I could send in my college application?" Owen said, throwing his hands up at the indignity of it all, "I mean, what year is it?"

Having grabbed a handful of what she sought, Kendra held them to her chest and went to the cash. Along the way she spotted something she'd recently read about.

"Oh wow, they sell these now!"

"What?" Owen asked.

"Well, um," Kendra lost her bluster, "these particular condoms were invented in the UK a while ago but it's taken years for them to be perfected. I guess they just came to America, like, a month ago. They change color when they come into contact with fluids containing an STD."

Owen picked a package off the wall and looked at the back. "Blue for syphilis, green for chlamydia…man, you knew about these already, huh?"

"Sure, yeah, I mean why not?" Kendra looked at the floor, tension creeping into her shoulders.

"No no, I think it's cool." Owen put the condoms back, "You're informed. It's a good way to be."

"I am!" Kendra, the three pack of condoms she'd hid in her jacket's inner pocket growing warm with the pride she felt, raised her head high, "I am very, very informed."

Soon the cashier was mumbling something inappropriate about how pleased he was to see a girl buying "such things" and "not just the boys". The colorful-haired conspirators shared a moment of mutual distaste while splitting the bill, then hurried back to Talib's house, the very first gusts of fall wind, and the

Red Bulls Owen bought, giving them wings.

Talib was back in the first floor den, trying his best to philosophize his way into the pants of the fourth and final drama club girl he'd invited. Kendra realized he hadn't invited any of the drama club boys. Up on the main floor, Camilla and the other two Gothic Lolitas were circled around Val. They all seemed fascinated by the story of how she'd stood up to Charlie at the play-structure.

"Would you really have fucked her dad?" Camilla asked, head turned in a way Kendra knew showed her approval. Val looked nervous, playing with the label of a bottle of beer one of the Lolitas had brought. Kendra remembered passing a girl crying on the front lawn. Had she been Camilla's prom date, and sorta-girlfriend, Lauren?

No time to think about that, Owen was already racing up to the top floor. On the way, Kendra had to push past Christopher. He was bragging to guys she didn't recognize, something about all the great blowjobs Mary had given him.

Seriously? Kendra thought, staring jeweled daggers with +3 against braggarts at him as she passed, *God dammit Mary, I'm gonna totally get better at-*

Thoughts were interrupted and things moved fast as Kendra felt Owen's hands grip her sides, lifting her up and over to the bend in the stairs. Two roughhousing rugby players and most of the railing crashed into the space where she'd been standing.

"Guys!" Owen said, "I know Talib's mom is gone for the evening but, guys, come on! Besides, you almost fell on Kendra, for Christ's sake."

Apologies were made, and accepted. Enough of the railing remained attached so the detached segment could be put back in place. It wouldn't stand to being leaned on, however it could pass a visual inspection well enough so the damage wouldn't be detected until after only Talib was left to take the rap. This was considered acceptable by all involved.

Owen and Kendra returned to the third floor. Nobody was in the bathroom, miracle of miracles, so they decided to start in there. Kendra locked the door, "Okay, let's do it."

Handing him the brown paper bag, Kendra watched as he removed a half dozen magazines promising the finest in exaggerated body parts colliding with each other.

"Oh, I got an idea," Owen said, "can you remove the last few tissues in that box on the counter?"

Kendra did, while Owen set about removing the annual subscription cards from the magazines, each one adorned with a visual sample of their title's contents. He then traded Kendra the magazines for the box, placing the subscription cards inside so they could be removed like the tissues it was made for.

"Amazing!" Kendra said, "I like how you built on my original idea. This is some good, you know, disruptive synergy we have going on here."

Pulling the curtain back, she asked Owen for the tape they'd picked up with the magazines. Pulling a large, four foot square poster from the folds of a magazine devoted to amateurs sending in pictures of themselves, Kendra decorated the inside of the shower. "Think we have enough butts up there?"

"Hmmm," Owen grabbed a second detachable centerfold from a magazine which proudly informed everyone that yes, these butts were extreme, "Maybe if we add this?"

"Excellent decision, Mr. Forster." Kendra began to imagine the pair of them as a power couple at parties in the future. Where was Owen going to school? She'd have to find out later.

Satisfied with the bathroom, they pulled the shower curtain closed and peeked into the hallway. Kendra thought she'd heard several people out there; it was empty now. The opportunity to mix in random pages of pornography with the motivational posters papering the walls was there for the taking. Laughter, taping, friendly shoulder nudges; the next five minutes were some of the best Kendra could remember having had all year.

"Okay," Owen said, "we have to put something extra nasty under Talib's pillow."

"The law requires it, surely." Kendra replied. Owen, bless his cotton socks, went ahead into Talib's uninhabited bedroom. Kendra came up close behind, pausing at the door for a moment. Once again she swore she heard a group of people; it was difficult to be sure. The other parts of the house were still full of party-goers and it's not like the stereo wasn't blasting in the living room. Seeing the shadow of someone coming up the stairs for the washroom, Kendra darted in and closed the door behind her.

Owen was giggling to himself with delight, having found an image featuring an impressive amount of enthusiastic activities worth giggling at. While he was focused on the task at hand, Kendra silently slid Talib's desk chair so it secured the door.

"Hah," Owen said, "talk about a 'two-page spread'."

Kendra looked, laughed, and leaned closer. Soon they were both laying on their elbows and knees, facing down at their latest masterpiece. Owen didn't need help removing the pages or slipping them under Talib's pillow like a tooth fairy who got kicked out of the academy. There was no good reason for her to get on the bed, so she didn't give him one.

Owen flipped up Talib's pillow and what he found, several sheets of graph paper with detailed drawings on them, caused the two of them to stifle screams of delight.

"Wow," he said, "these are better than anything we've put up."

Talib had meticulously drawn, with minimal artistic skill, dozens of nude women baring breasts capable of feeding entire maternity wards and wearing lion's manes of hair looking like they'd been cut from plexiglass. Kendra couldn't help smirking. These women were mostly made of curved lines, so why had he drawn them on graph paper?

"Look, I think we can both agree those were awesome, so awesome, and we'll be having some words with Talib about them, sooner or later." Kendra brought the pillow back down, drawing his attention back to the centerfold, "But, first things first..."

"Gotcha."

Owen didn't notice the change in Kendra caused by his closeness. Not wanting to tear the two-page titillation he still wanted to slip under Talib's pillow, he was focused on carefully removing staples. It wasn't like being in the woods with Will. Any fear of what might come next was drowned under a swirling sea of alcohol and amorousness, a time-honored technique.

"Here, uh, just let me help you," Kendra began to feel a little dizzy, "with, um…"

Her mouth molded against his. She had no idea how to describe the way his beard felt, just that it was wonderful and suitably beard-like. A curl of his mustache threatened to tickle the inside of her nostril. Taking advantage of their unsteady positioning, she jostled Owen onto his back and stole a second kiss.

Kiss Owen, She thought, *K.O.! And he is a knock-out. If I kiss him a third time then that'd be a T.K.O. maybe? Or maybe that would mean three knockouts, three Owens-*

Owen grabbing her by the shoulders, holding her in place above him. Kendra didn't get her third K.O.

"Kendra, hold up." He'd already put on a face, a kinder version of one she remembered Will wearing in the woods, "I'm sorry if I led you on. I don't-"

Eyebrows narrowing, Kendra writhed in his grip. Grabbing one thick wrist with both her hands, she tried to force his fingers down her pants and up between her legs. Really, she wanted to reach deep inside of him, to find the switch or dial or button to press so he'd think of her the way she wanted him to.

"Kendra!"

She gave up on Owen's hand and pushed forward, pressing her chest against his, getting her T.K.O. Later, she wondered how she'd managed to overpower, even briefly, a man who weighed at least eighty pounds more than her. It wouldn't be until she was much older that Kendra would realize raw physical strength wasn't the only factor in play.

He did, however, manage to re-establish some space between them, "Kendra, Jesus! Consent!"

"What are you talking about? Boys are, like, 80% consent and 20% water!" Sitting back on his pelvis, Kendra slapped her hands down on her thighs, "God, why won't anybody…I mean, nobody ever, *ever*…"

"Oh, you've never…?" Owen relaxed a little, "I heard Gwen say something earlier and figured she was just being a bitch." He reached for her hips, to try and move her; Kendra shoved his hands away and sat down harder.

"Gwen doesn't have to lie to be a bitch." Kendra tried to press forward, Owen catching her by the shoulders again, "Owen! You get with all these girls, what the hell is your problem?"

"What the hell is *my* problem?" Owen yelled before, Kendra guessed, counting to ten and slowing his breath, "Okay, you're angry, I feel you."

Kendra raised an eyebrow.

"Look, I never felt great about hitting that guy. He had problems and I wasn't helping. It's just, the day before, I told my parents I didn't want to go into computer engineering or programming when I finished school." Owen scowled, "So they bought a sick SUV with the money they'd set aside for my education."

"That's shitty, Owen, seriously it is," Kendra stopped pushing forward, letting her upper body hang there in Owen's hands, "but what's it got to do with me?"

"Well, so I didn't want to become what they wanted me to become and I wasn't sure what I did want to be. I just knew I didn't want to be angry and feel like crap about myself." Owen carefully pushed Kendra back until she was sitting upright again, "So I tried to take better care of myself, channeling all my angry energy into exercise, to not let anything inside stop me from experimenting with different ways of presenting myself, and to, you know, go after what I wanted."

"Owen, that doesn't really…" Kendra looked away, "You're kind of babbling nonsense."

"I'm saying, feeling crazy's no excuse for acting crazy, you know? Instead, I found a way to be happier and more confident by, you know, learning to be myself. I shouldn't need to tell you of all people."

"Are you for real?" Kendra crossed her arms, staring right down the barrel of Owen's irises, "I've been 'being myself' like a motherfucker and it's done me no damn good, not a fuckin'-"

"Well, why don't you just-"

"It's not about 'being yourself' it's about good looks. You just did the guy version of letting your hair down and taking your glasses off you dumb-"

"I mean, there's gotta be at least a few guys who'd sleep with you."

"At least a few? Wow, thanks."

"Well, I mean if getting laid is so important to you."

"Says the guy who's slept with how many girls since he lost some fat and found some fashion? Who got a little confidence?" Kendra snapped, "Listen, who you sleep with the first time? It's a bigger deal for girls."

Owen looked unsure of this.

Kendra thought for a moment, then breathed out. “How about I show you what I mean?”

He didn’t look any more confident.

“Look, I know it’s a lot to ask after the last two minutes, but can I ask you to trust me?”

“Uh, alright.”

“Stick out the index finger on your right hand.”

Owen did.

“Okay, now stick it in the space between the pillow and the mattress.”

Reaching behind his head, he did.

“Good, now put the same finger in the space between Talib’s mattress and the…boxspring? Bedframe? Whatever it’s called.”

Bringing his hand over and down, he did.

“Okay, now maybe…” Kendra grabbed a baseball cap off Talib’s bedside table. She folded the hat like a taco and held it in front of Owen. He took the hint, putting his finger in there. After a long moment, Kendra gestured to let him know he could take his finger out.

“You can relax your hand. Now,” she told him, “let me put my index finger deep inside your mouth. Right up to the first knuckle.”

“What?” Owen replied, “No way!”

Kendra shifted back and punched down between her legs, right into Owen’s crotch. Owen folded in half, pinching Kendra between his chest and knees. Scrambling sideways, she fell to the floor with all the grace and poise of a cat escaping a dunk in the bath.

Kendra hadn't intentionally hit a boy there since early grade school. During the time between blows, the very idea of doing such a thing had become like Talib's drawings, funny, harmless, and cartoonishly divorced from reality. Seeing Owen wince, unable to catch his breath, this didn't feel like any of that.

Getting up, she removed the chair from the door and looked back at Owen.

"Well," she said, shaky with adrenaline, "maybe that'll help you remember it's a bigger deal to have someone inside you than to put yourself inside someone else!"

She didn't feel as tough as her words. She didn't care. All Kendra wanted to do now was find Valory, pull the ripcord, and parachute away from this party like the fiery disaster it was bound to become when Owen recovered and told people what she'd done.

Stepping into the hall she saw a line for the bathroom, leading back to the stairs. Closing the door behind her, nobody seemed to notice Owen. Kendra noticed something, though, when she heard a similar noise to the one from earlier and finally recognized it; Valory's voice, muffled and coming from Talib's mother's bedroom. Turning to her right, Kendra shoved the door wide open, hoping her friend was okay.

Shadows. Legs. Hands. Eyes. Mouths. Tongues. Worse. A horrible confluence of creatures.

It was uncanny.

It was Richard, Valory, and Camilla, all on the bed. Some

items of clothing were on the floor. Everyone seemed to want to be there. Richard and Camilla were extra keen to be with Valory, Kendra's friend who'd always said she was as alone as her.

"You've been fuckin' lying…about fucking, haven't you?!?" Kendra bellowed, "I mean, Richard AND Camilla? You've been having ALL the sex!"

Three sets of eyes in the bedroom were staring at her; one pair beginning to cry. Kendra jammed her forearms against either side of the door frame, fists shaking as she tried to collapse the house around them.

"And Richard…is this why you've been so damn…Lauren? Camilla, why did you even?" Kendra stomped her foot, hard, "Bitch, is this why you helped me with Will? Some long con to get close to…Jesus, shit!"

Valory tried to apologize; Kendra didn't give her the chance. Stomping past the audience she wished would just die or vanish or something, Kendra kept cursing out her three friends as she approached the stairs. The timing of a foul, multi-syllable assault against Camilla could have been better, as it was unleashed right beside Yasu, one Gothic Lolita whose name Kendra could finally remember.

"Hey," Yasu said, moving to block Kendra's path, "you can't talk that way about my friend. Apologize."

"Eat twelve thousand dicks with a spoon!" Kendra replied, trying to shove her way past. Three seconds of frantic grappling between her and Yasu led to Kendra spinning around, then stumbling backwards down the stairs. She reached out to catch the railing, the same one which had been put back into place with less than a quarter of its legs still attached. Most of the railing slid off to hang over the lower side of the stairwell, with Kendra tumbling after.

The stair's soft carpeting was little comfort as she bumped and slid down. Head thumping against the floor, Kendra gasped before opening her eyes to get an upside-down view of Tim and Celine. She was glad to see he'd gotten her some water, then forgot all about it when she realized why they were staring. In the struggle with Yasu a button had come undone and, while falling down the stairs, her jacket had been pulled open wide enough to flash everyone.

A rugby player tried to help her up. Kendra shoved out of his grasp before she was even standing; darting downstairs just as Talib was coming to see what all the commotion was about.

"Kendra, what are-"

"Would all of you just get out my way," She scrambled around him, "please!"

Missing a step on her way to the ground floor, Kendra nearly lost her balance again. Reaching the front door, she looked up the stairs at Talib's concerned face, then into the den where the last drama girl was doing up shirt buttons, staring back at her. Kendra, despite herself, wanted to shout something at Talib about how "love found a way".

Yanking open the door, she stepped past Lauren and her tears, then shot off into the night, driving her body like she stole it.

The Bridge

Weaving. Dodging. Alleys. Hopping fences. Street light halos. Cracked concrete hitting hard against soft soled shoes. A coppery taste forming in the back of a throat that felt shredded.

"Fuck. You!" Kendra yelled at her body, "It hasn't been that long since I stopped running, you piece of shit."

She raked her nails over her chest, drawing white lines down across the blue ones painted earlier. She was lost; it was soothing. Seeing something familiar would force her onto a long slow path back to her world, a place she never wanted to see again. Turning a corner she worried would bring her back somewhere she'd recognize, Kendra literally stopped on a dime.

"What?" Kendra laughed, looking down at the coin poking out from under her foot, "Amazing."

Picking it up, she forgot everything else for a moment. Then, the image of what she saw in Talib's mother's bedroom flashed across her mind like a slide of crushed kittens mixed in with family vacation photos. She yelped, snapping her head to the side, throwing the dime in the same direction. Opening her eyes again, Kendra couldn't tell where it had gone other than Somewhere In Those Super Tall Noise Canceling Hedges. Noise-canceling hedges? Turning her head the other way, she realized she was near the highway. There was a small bridge going over it, leading in the opposite direction of the neighborhoods she knew.

Blood sugar and adrenaline levels all over the map, Kendra marched herself toward the bridge. Linear time began to feel like it wouldn't apply if only she was there.

Yes, please, Kendra thought. It wasn't just blood chemistry and exhaustion making it difficult for her to move. Dragging the ghostly chains of her own judgments and expectations, she ached under the burden.

"Got a K.O., kissed Owen, I guess." She said, her voice swinging between anger and melancholy, "But I didn't get an O.K., he didn't kiss me, I kissed on him even after he made it clear he didn't want me to and that's not okay."

An eighteen-wheeler blew past her, swinging left to go down the on-ramp. It pulled the air along with it, sending a powerful gust against Kendra's back. She stood still, grimacing, waiting for the sensation to pass. A full minute went by before she looked both ways, then crossed the on-ramp to reach the start of the bridge. She fetishized the middle of the bridge as a haven. Her mouth began to move again.

"Well gee Kevin, that was just so nice of you to be a meathead and a maniac," She stopped, resting against the chain-link fence atop the stubby concrete barrier between her and dropping down to the highway, "well gee Scott Allison, well gee boy at the pool that one time, well gee Will Daniels, well gee fuckin' Paul, well gee Owen…"

The fence pressed deeper into Kendra's clenched fingers as she bent down to face the sidewalk.

"What the FUCK Valory?" She screamed, bile rising up her esophagus. A drop of spit fell to feed a few blades of grass creeping through a crack, "I mean, is this it? Is this what I get?"

Chest heaving, Kendra pulled herself back upright. The middle, she was so close to the middle of the bridge.

Then she was there. Keeping her eyes closed, both hands hanging from the fence, she brought her head back up as if to admire the sky. She tried to reach out with her mind to summon the sensation which had driven her to tears just the other night, of timelessness and isolation from everything.

"Come on," She growled, "I want it now. I want it. Don't let anybody touch me…not touch me…"

A few deep breaths. Nothing. She opened her eyes, looked around. Black sky, yellow lights, grey concrete. Like a sinus infection left untreated, Kendra felt a painful pressure behind her eyes and forehead as she tried to reconcile all the theories, hers and others, with actual lived experience.

"Stop it." She closed her eyes again, "This doesn't make any sense. What am I-"

Like a dozen overlapping radio channels overpowered by the electronic tinnitus of a high-pitched signal whine, Kendra's thoughts cut out.

She began to climb the fence.

An awning of chain link angled back from the top, showing no signs of razor wire or other deterrents. Confident she could manage, Kendra continued up. Every few steps she'd stop, staring down at the traffic. It was sparse this time of night. She'd have to time it perfectly. A few feet more and she had to work out how to climb around the awning. Hanging by her hands, she began to swing her legs left and right to gain momentum, a pendulum trying to become a period, full stop.

A hand grabbed her ankle. Kendra screamed.

"Jesus Kendra, it's me!"

"Steve?"

"I'm not letting go," He was so stern, so serious, she couldn't recognize the dumb boy she'd seen hang out with her brother, "so you can come down with me or wiggle out of my grasp and fall back onto the bridge. You'll just hurt yourself and have to go to the hospital. Have fun explaining that to your mom."

"Oh shit," Kendra said, looking back up, away from Steve, "I forgot about mom and dad."

"Well uh," he'd seemingly exhausted a prepared speech, "you coming down or what?"

Kendra nodded. Soon they both stood by the car she hadn't heard him drive up alongside, its engine still humming, large round headlights, shocked by all they saw.

"So," Steve said, "I guess you turned your phone off."

Kendra stared at her phone, its screen blank. She had no memory of doing that. As if speaking to her cold black rectangle, she asked "So, uh…you…found me?"

"Track and field did its thing; nobody at the party could even come close to catching up with you." Steve continued, "When Val couldn't get you on your phone, she called Greg to say you were in trouble and gone off to God knows where. He called me and some of the guys. Asked us to help look for you."

Kendra scrunched up her face, “Really?”

“Yeah, Kendra. I know he can be a dick sometimes but he still cares about you.” Steve shook his head, “Anyways, I was passing under the bridge when I heard someone yelling something and it was you. Thank God it isn't hard to loop back here from the next on-ramp or I might have been-”

Steve put his hands on her shoulders, “Listen, can we please get in my car? I'd feel much more comfortable.”

“Okay.” Kendra answered, “I don't want to go anywhere, I want to stay here.”

Steve looked at her, then walked Kendra to the passenger side. As he went back around to get in, she admired the tasteless, cream-colored fake fur he'd covered the seats with. A few seconds spent stroking this, pretending to be Kendrella giving orders to her ship, was a welcome micro-break.

“Were you seriously gonna try and kill yourself?” Steve asked, settling into the driver's seat.

“When you're in my situation, being told you have your whole life ahead of you feels more like a threat than anything.” Kendra wanted to cry, didn't let herself, “I'm sorry. God, I feel like a crazy person.”

“Hey, Kendra, it's okay.”

“It's not okay! Nobody I want ever wants me!”

Steve, looking thoughtful, went quiet. As he took a time out, Kendra took him in. He was a young man now, blond hair combed back like some yuppie stockbroker, a weathered black leather jacket he must have inherited or bought second hand, aviator shades hanging in the V of a t-shirt turned off-white by a casual disregard for sorting laundry, and deep blue jeans he filled out nicely.

"Listen, Kay, I hated being a virgin too." Steve said, "I get where you're coming from."

"When you're thirteen and a bunch of girls pay the hottest guy in school to ask you out as a joke," Kendra shuddered, nails digging into her thighs, "when your opportunities are so few and the stakes always so high; when people tell you you're the gatekeeper of boy's urges and then someone you thought was a good friend proves them right; when you have to learn how to fend off Internet creeps by yourself since your parents just assume they have nothing to teach you about computers because you grew up with them; when you want to be looked at and not looked at and looked at and not looked at; when boys get compliments for being willing to go down on something as 'gross' as a pussy, but you'd get an entire scarlet alphabet if you told anyone you'd like to lick a dick like an ice cream cone; when the biggest loser in school has a boyfriend and she gets to have sex with him while you sit at home trying to remember what it felt like to steal a kiss from someone who didn't want you; when you crave sex but your body won't cooperate and it doesn't matter anyways because nobody wants to cooperate with you; when you keep trying to be good because you think it'll make good things come to you, and yeah maybe sometimes, but never the things you're really hoping for; when you know a bridge isn't high enough for the fall to kill you, so you work out the timing to fall in front of a car doing twenty over the limit; when there's apparently some whole secret universe where your best friend has relationships with two of your other friends, and even though it's not what you want, you wish you were included just so you could touch and be touched, just so you could feel less excluded from a world woven out of what you want every minute of the damn day, out of a desire you'd be sad to escape even if you could get away from it; then, then you'll get where I'm coming from!"

Steve felt her breath as she caught it. Then she inhaled his. Neither of them knew who started kissing who. Kendra couldn't believe the cliché of it all. She didn't care. For the first time in her life she was kissing with someone, not on them. Still, after a short forever, she had questions.

"Wait a second? What the hell? I thought you thought I was ugly."

"What?"

"Let me see if I can remember." Kendra brought an index finger to her chin with mock theatricality, "I think it was something like 'Spaghetti legs, spaghetti arms, not much ass, not a lot of tits - happy tits, though!'"

Steve covered his face with both hands, "Ah, geez."

"'Hair like a librarian…' and so on." Kendra pulled apart his hands so she could look him in the eyes, "Tell me Steve, is my face still 'kind of a medium'?"

"I'm so sorry for that bullshit." He answered, "I thought you were cute, I have for so long. I dunno, it was weird with you being Greg's sister. I wasn't sure what would happen if I admitted it. I just-"

Kendra put a finger to his lips. She wasn't as smooth as she'd hoped, the tip slipping through to rest on his front teeth. She just needed a second to process, damn it. Steve gently moved her hand to her lap as she did so.

"So, what do you-"

"Shhh," Kendra kissed him, enjoying feeling in charge of the situation, "it's okay, you were young and dumb."

Steve tried to suggest they at least bring the car out from under the streetlight, if not head somewhere else entirely. Kendra smothered his words with her tongue. Part of her wanted to be caught, to show someone proof how, for once, the current of desire wasn't flowing in a single direction.

Their lips, hands, kissed, clutched, built a bridge for her, between a wilderness of wonderings and the acres of answers found across it. After a while, Kendra thought about the warm place her wanderlust was walking her towards. Having become lost, almost dying, along the way only made its pull more powerful.

There were those condoms in her jacket, and she could let him drive them somewhere they wouldn't be interrupted. Even if she might have backed out at that last second she'd been so close to, when he grabbed her ankle, Steve had just saved her from herself. She didn't owe him anything. Was gratefulness such bad motivation? What other boy had ever done such a thing for her?

I could even be all clever, She thought, *And say 'So, would you fuck her?' just like dumbass said to the other guys, way back when.*

Way back, when he hadn't had the confidence to say he thought she was cute. When he tried to use a committee to determine if it was acceptable to like her. When he'd been asked if he'd fuck her and must have either said 'No', or 'Yeah, if…' followed by some caveat of her looking different or maybe just the punchline to a crude, stupid joke at her expense.

Yeah, no. Kendra thought, *Not with Steve, personal deadlines be damned.*

Besides, she didn't feel the same as she had before they'd begun kissing. It wasn't losing her virginity; it was plenty for now. Still, Kendra couldn't help shoving her hand down to give a powerful squeeze before, worried she wouldn't let go if she lingered, she pulled all of herself back to herself, pushing deep into her side of the car. Steve looked confused. She was glad to see he wasn't angry.

"Steve I don't want to tease or anything, but I think this is as far as I want to go with you."

"Uhm, okay." Steve settled back against the inside of the driver's side door, "Like, ever?"

"Yeah, ever." Kendra bit her lower lip, "Sorry."

She didn't want to go around being terrified of men. She also didn't want to be beaten, raped, or murdered.

"Aw, you sure?" He gave a small smile, "I mean, I respect it, it's just not what I was hoping for. You know what I mean. Your body, though, not mine."

"Thanks Steve," She wanted to give him another kiss, even another squeeze, "for not being, you know, terrible."

Not seeming to catch the seriousness of what she was alluding to, he just laughed, "No problem. I'll try not to be terrible in the future, either. No more 'medium face'."

Kendra put on her seatbelt and let out a long sigh of relief, "Yeah, no more 'medium face'."

Steve pulled up into her parent's driveway. She was glad they were still away on date night. Given the hour, it was possible her father had gotten them a fancy hotel room. It was nice to be trusted with the house all to herself. Briefly thinking about inviting Steve inside, Kendra dismissed the idea with far less difficulty than if she'd had it back on the bridge.

"Thanks again, I'll let everyone know I'm okay before I go to bed."

"Good. I'll tell your brother right now, though. I already feel bad for not having texted him as soon as you were in the car."

"Okay, good night!"

Steve looked like he expected one last kiss, maybe on the cheek. Kendra thought about it, chose to run her hand along the left line of his chin and step out of the car without saying another word. The sound of his pulling away and driving down the street was soon replaced by dogs barking. Honey Garlic and Spicy Italian were both at the front window, excited to see her.

Guh, I shouldn't have thanked him for not being horrible. Not being horrible shouldn't earn you a cookie. Kendra paused, *Well, of the mis-steps I made tonight it's hardly the worst one.*

Kendra picked up her stride and went indoors.

"Mark! Mark! Mark!" Honey Garlic said.

"Oh yeah?" Kendra replied.

"Mrrrrrrruffff!" Spicy Italian added.

"I see, I see." Kendra, leaving the lights off, found her way over to her mother's favorite chair. Sunk deep into the cushion was Salvador Doggy, following her progress with his weary, old eyes. Kendra crouched down, running her fingers from his head to his tail, over and over. Honey and Spicy settled against the base of the chair. This tableau stayed still until Kendra buried her face into the short hairs of Salvador's back. Not knowing what to do about the hard, wet, sobbing coming from their master, the three dachshunds did what they could - they stayed close.

"I'm not-" She cried a while longer, before continuing, "I'm going away to school soon and I'm probably not going to be here. I'm probably not going to be here when you die. I'm sorry, I'm so sorry."

Again and again Kendra apologized to Salvador. The bubble she'd sought on the bridge, a separation from time and space, formed around her and the little life she knew was nearing the end of its run. She wished they never had to leave it.

Her crying distressed the younger two dogs and they joined her, howling in solidarity. The moment with Salvador intruded upon, Kendra got up and took him with her. Gold and blue glitter on her cheeks glinted in the moonlight, tears having spread them further apart, like stars in an aging universe. She couldn't help it, she had to laugh.

"Oh Jesus," Kendra looked down at Spicy and Honey, excited now she was standing again, as if this might lead to a game, "You guys, you little guys."

Spicy and Honey stayed in the living room, waiting for a ball to be brought back for them to fight over, watched Kendra carry their father up the stairs and into her room.

She made a little nest in her bedsheets, placing her beloved old dog at the heart of it. Satisfied, she let out another long sigh, feeling sober once more. Salvador, in total silence and keeping his eyes on Kendra, accepted everything.

"I guess seventeen is pretty damn good for a dog, eh pup?" She said, then rubbed her face with both hands, "Ugh, okay, I can't think about this anymore. Not right now."

Still wanting moonlight, Kendra didn't touch any of her bedroom lamps. She closed her door and, using the mirror hanging from it, undid a series of snarls, her hair falling to her collarbone. Kendra hung up her jacket and put on a Gordon Coles University t-shirt her father, beaming with pride, bought her when they'd visited the campus two weeks back. At the time Kendra had felt embarrassed, had tried to explain she'd long ago ceased to enjoy wearing clothes advertising places she'd been. Now she hugged herself and the shirt, then went over and gave Salvador an even firmer hug.

"Oh geez, I gotta let people know what's up." Kendra turned to lay on one side, facing Salvador, and woke up her phone.

An orchestra of notification sounds heralded the arrival of Spicy and Honey. Wondering what the delay was with this ball situation, they'd come up the stairs. Running over to the edge of the bed, both struggled to get up and onto the mattress. Kendra chuckled as she put a palm under each of their butts for a quick lift. Then she sent out a group text to Camilla, Celine, Richard, Tim, and Val to let them know she was safe, asking them to let anybody else who cared know they could stop worrying about her.

"Okay, wow," She turned to the two younger dogs, "looks like you guys arrived just in time for some stories."

Kendra, using an avalanche of guilt-ridden texts from close friends, stitched together a tale for Salvador and his children.

"Well," She began, putting on her best fairy godmother voice, "it seems Val and Richard, after that scary stuff in the market two years ago, well I guess the fear of death or injury really can be an aphrodisiac. They took each other's virginity and then dated for about a year, when Richard broke things off because... okay, it seems he was mad Val insisted they keep it a secret. Oh...oh...yup, there's some texts from Richard confirming this and he apologizes, then tries to make some old Dicklegs jokes because too much sincerity always makes him nervous...then Val..."

Kendra read in silence for a moment.

"She thought I'd feel totally alone and horrible if I found out she was no longer a virgin." Kendra looked up from her phone, "Man, paving roads and good intentions and all that, eh doggies? God, I love her so much."

"Hmm, Camilla says her friendship is genuine...she helped me with Will mostly because she liked me and partly because she thought it was better for him to just move on instead of doing long distance with Azealia, but she also had this huge crush on Val and wasn't sure how to navigate the Richard thing, Val... having trouble making peace with...okay I'm not going to put it as crudely as Cammy does, but basically Val was wrestling with being bisexual." Val put her phone down, "And somehow this all led to the tangle of terribleness I saw tonight."

Turning on a light, Kendra went to her desk and removed the disposable contacts she'd bought for the party. Putting her glasses on, she picked up her phone and called Steve.

"Hey, I need to ask a favor. Would you mind picking me up and taking me back to the party?"

"No problem. You sure, though?"

"Yeah, I've got some questions and apologies to sort out and I want to do it now, in person, before I lose my nerve."

"Okay, I'll be there soon."

"Thanks Steve." Kendra grinned, "You're, like, a medium guy."

Steve laughed and hung up.

Kendra looked around her room. She'd given up all hope of ever seeing the little creatures her younger, still-developing brain had placed in its shadows, and the only pile of men's clothes ever found by the bed had been her own. However there were new rooms, boys, and challenges to be found.

Sex? Kendra thought, *It'll come when it comes.*

"Ha ha," She said out loud, "come."

Epilogue

Wrapped up in her vintage nautical coat, a prize from the markets near Gordon Coles University, Kendra stood in her parents backyard as snow swept down from the clouds. Back inside, her family was having a spirited discussion about who should set the table for Christmas Eve dinner. She didn't care, all of her attention was on the large stone her mother had set at the end of the garden.

"Hello Salvador," Kendra said to the stone, "I'm home for the holidays and there's something I don't really want to share with everyone yet, but I thought I'd share it with you."

A pause. Kendra felt silly. Pushing a lock of firetruck red hair away from her face, she bit the inside of her cheek just hard enough to sting, holding on until the feeling passed.

"So I'll tell you a story," She smiled, "Two days ago a girl met a boy, the night before she had to get a train back to visit her family for Christmas. Well, they'd technically met at the start of the school year when she began her Politics and Globalization class, they just hadn't spoken before."

Kendra drew a semi-circle in the snow with her foot, then continued.

"Anyways, they met and they shared a feeling. Later, in her

dorm room, they shared each other." Kendra's mother texted her to come inside for dinner, "Man, I wish I could…I mean a girl…whatever, I wish I could text you, Salvador. Me and my texting ghost-doggy, wouldn't it be awesome?"

"So yeah, maybe I'll have a boyfriend when I get back from holidays, maybe not. I dunno, I'm just glad to feel on the other side of something. The side I was on wasn't as bad as I thought, but damn it feels good to leave it behind." Kendra turned around to face the house, continuing to talk to Salvador as she headed back, "You know, it didn't happen because I'd figured out the perfect set of rules to follow, and it didn't unlock any secrets of the universe or anything. I only know what it was like to have sex with that one boy, in that one way, in that one time, in the one place.

It's more than I knew before, though, and that's what matters to me."

ACKNOWLEDGMENTS

Thanks to Jacqueline Hoffman, Jamie Kipp, Christina Manuge, and Anna Sharret for reading my early drafts, as well as Avril McMeekins for her excellent story editing work. I'm also grateful to Aquapunkchick for their enthusiastic encouragement online, Sasha for all her loving support, and my parents for everything.

Big thanks to Toronto's own *Merril Collection of Science Fiction, Speculation & Fantasy* for being such a wonderful place to write & do research.

KENDRA'S READING LIST

In case you're curious to check out one of the books Kendra is shown reading, here they all are.

The Godfather by Mario Puzo
The Left Hand of Darkness by Ursula K. LeGuin
Oryx & Crake by Margaret Atwood
Clan of the Cave Bear by Jean Auel
Bear by Marian Engel
A Mind of Its Own: A Cultural History of the Penis by David Friedman

ABOUT THE AUTHOR

Oliver Brackenbury is an author and screenwriter. He grew up around the corner from a five-story deep nuclear fallout shelter, as one does, and can now be found living not far from a popular 1,815.4 ft tower in Toronto. Teenage Oliver most certainly did NOT write twenty pages of a novel about Basically-Him and Basically-A-Girl-He-Liked having adventures in the post-apocalyptic ruins of his home town.

His first novel, JUNKYARD LEOPARD, came out in 2015 through the Bad Day Books imprint of Assent Publications. In 2016 it was deemed worthy of inclusion in the *The Merril Collection of Science Fiction, Speculation and Fantasy*, which also holds horror titles.

OLIVER
BRACKENBURY
IS…

ONLINE

You can learn more about him and his work at www.oliverbrackenbury.com, or follow him at...

Twitter: https://tinyletter.com/oliverbrackenbury

Instagram: https://www.instagram.com/obracken/

Goodreads: https://www.goodreads.com/oliverbrackenbury

Goodreads and Amazon reviews honestly do help, so if you liked the book please let people know!

Facebook: https://www.facebook.com/brackenbooks

and

Tumblr: http://igotopinions.com

Meanwhile, *BWSG* is my magazine-style newsletter that goes out roughly four times a year and often includes new fiction, as well as the inside scoop on what I'm up to: https://tinyletter.com/oliverbrackenbury

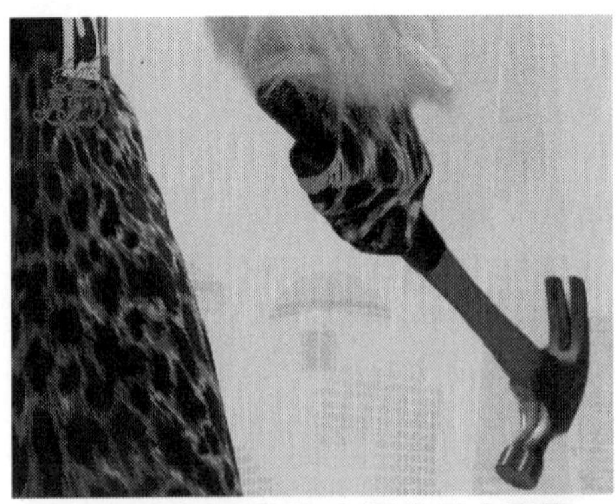

JUNKYARD LEOPARD

A NOVEL BY OLIVER BRACKENBURY

A leopard-print silhouette crossed the street in an arc, like an ellipsis closing off a horrible, private thought.

Mary is a young woman who's unaware she's dealing with her anxiety by putting on a costume and slaughtering corrupt Wall Street bankers.

She only wants to be happy.

She was wearing a short, white fur coat and a belt with type on it he had only begun to read when the butt of a power drill was driven into his forehead, the bit already spinning.

This was not the end of Tony's discomfort.

Oliver Brackenbury's debut novel offers gore-slicked catharsis for anyone struggling to get by.

www.junkyardleopard.com